BASEBALL SPY

BASEBALL SPY

SCOTT REISTER

YOUNG
DRAGONS

YOUNG
DRAGONS

an imprint of
Roan & Weatherford Publishing Associates, LLC
Bentonville, Arkansas

Library of Congress Cataloging-in-Publication Data
Names: Reister, Scott, author
Title: Baseball Spy/Scott Reister | Sports Spy #1
Description: First Edition | Bentonville: Young Dragons, 2023
Identifiers: LCCN: 2024932931 | ISBN: 978-1-63373-885-0 (trade paperback) |
ISBN: 978-1-63373-886-7 (eBook)
Subjects: JUVENILE FICTION/Spies & Spying |
JUVENILE FICTION/Action & Adventure |
JUVENILE FICTION/Sports & Recreation/Baseball & Softball
LC record available at: https://lccn.loc.gov/2024932931

Young Dragons trade paperback edition April, 2024

Cover & Interior Design by Casey W. Cowan
Editing by George "Clay" Mitchell, Amy Cowan & Lisa Lindsey

To Allyson, Mallory, Ryan, and Sammy,
who REALLY wanted me to tell him
who the spy was.

ACKNOWLEDGMENTS

THANK YOU TO all my family members that read the early versions of this story and kept up the encouragement. Librarians Julie Finch and Kayla Becker helped me with invaluable feedback and editing when they barely knew me. Incredible authors Josh Berk and Tracey Garvis-Graves were wonderful resources and very gracious with their time. Thank you to my enthusiastic agent/cheerleader Jessica Reino and Metamorphosis Literary Agency for loving the book, the endless support, and bringing it into this world. Editor George "Clay" Mitchell and publishers Casey and Amy Cowan at Roan & Weatherford Publishing/ Young Dragons Press wanted the book and shaped the final product into what you are holding today. They are the best at what they do. Thank you all. It takes a village!

AUTHOR'S NOTE

WHEN I WAS a kid playing sports, I fantasized the fate of the world depended on…me! Whether or not I made the play was truly a life-or-death situation, so I better not screw up. But what if that situation really happened? *Could* it really happen? You're about to find out. And remember: Losing is *NOT* an option.

RENEGADES LINEUP
(sometimes)

STARTERS
#1 SS Braxton Greiner
#9 LF Ricky Martinez
#0 1B Erik Olsson
#15 P Dorian Delini
#10 C Sammy Logan
#9 CF Zane Mitchell
#8 3B Amber Hyatt
#3 RF Mateo Perez
#16 2B Jamal Atwater

BENCH
#2 OF Teddy Rempke
#19 IF Yuri Sokolov
#7 2B/P Cedric Atwater

MANAGER: Paul "Rudy" Rudella
COACHES: Ches Logan, Victor Perez

LEAGUE: Hillandale Little League 14U
RECORD: Not great

CHAPTER 1

WHERE *WAS* SHE? True, he broke the door, screamed, and even told her not to come, but never in a million years did Zane Mitchell think he'd be standing here, in the final inning, still wondering whether or not his mom was going to show. This summer she had pledged to stop traveling so much, be more present, and come to every one of his games. It's a promise Zane needed, and one his mom, Mallory Clayborn, had kept.

Until today.

The crack of the bat brought him back. It was an easy fly, a "can of corn" as his dad used to say. Zane drifted to his left and was about to call off Teddy Rempke, the Renegades' right fielder. But Teddy was running in hard.

"I got—" Teddy started to say.

Zane backed off.

Teddy froze.

Thunk.

The ball came down like a giant raindrop getting sucked

in by the moist grass. Zane pounced on it and rifled the ball to his cutoff man, but the runner from third was already crossing home for the Aces to tie the game. Zane saw the horror in his fellow outfielder's face as he felt everyone staring in their direction.

"What was that?!" Dorian Delini shouted from the pitcher's mound. He threw his hands up to drive the point home. Dorian had been acting like that all game, which only made Zane feel better about his decision. He could at least help Teddy save face.

"My bad!" Zane called back. He tapped his hand to his chest, taking ownership of Teddy's costly mistake. Dorian shook his head with disgust and spun back to the mound.

Rudy stepped out of the dugout and whistled. "Hey! We're still in this thing. Let's just get out of this inning."

Zane looked back at the shiny, half-filled aluminum bleachers, disappointment slowly turning into anger. She decided to stay home, just to prove a point. The fact she would act like that really hurt. At this rate, he wouldn't even mind that embarrassing "Let's go Zane-a-Lane" chant. The way things had been going, he would have welcomed it.

Being the new guy would have been easier for Zane if he had been playing even half as well as he had last summer. There would have been instant respect. But to these kids, Zane was just some guy that showed up in the middle of the season and didn't get hits when they needed them. Zane wanted to make friends, but four weeks had gone by, and he stopped trying. Some of the kids were okay, but others were flat-out jerks. Zane was too nervous to start up any conversations, and Dorian and his buddies were more than happy acting like Zane didn't exist.

The only one who had it worse was Amber Hyatt. Her only fault was being a girl who wanted to play on a team of boys. Shortstop Braxton Greiner and first baseman Erik Olsson copied Dorian, acting visibly annoyed any time she made a mistake. This, in turn, intimidated everybody else and caused even more tension. Now it was Zane's turn to get caught in the middle of it all.

Maybe Zane could redeem himself. He got to his ready position in center. Just like Rudy preached, he was careful to keep his hands on his thighs, not on his knees. He went over the situation in his head. It was the bottom of the seventh and final inning—unless the team could get another out and force extras. He told himself, "Whatever you do, no more mistakes."

His next chance came immediately. The batter put a perfect swing on the ball, smashing it deep to center. Zane's only chance was to turn and sprint straight back. As he approached the chain-link fence, he began to stumble. He looked back at the sky but couldn't locate the ball. He stuck out his lanky arm as far as he could as he fell forward.

And caught it.

"Yeah!" yelled Teddy.

Zane heard the screams from the crowd as he stared at his glove in amazement.

Teddy jogged over to congratulate Zane. "Nice!"

Zane got up slowly, enjoying the moment. He held up the ball and dusted his pants. He waved back at his teammates, who were still shouting things.

Urgently.

"Throw it!"

"Runner!"

Zane looked up at the field. That was only out number two.

The inning wasn't over.

The runner on second had tagged and was already rounding third, taking advantage of the few seconds gained by Zane's mental error. Zane quickly threw the ball in, but he already knew what was about to happen. All that was left to do was watch the winning run trot home. Ball game. The rest of the Aces zipped out of the dugout to celebrate.

Erik threw down his glove on first base. "Are you freaking *kidding* me?"

Zane looked over at Teddy. "I thought that was the last out."

Teddy gave him a half smile, not sure what to say. Zane took a deep breath and began to slink off the field with his teammates.

He went over to Dorian. "Sorry, man. I thought—"

Dorian cut him off. "Don't talk to me."

"Dorian," Amber said, bounding in. "How many guys did you walk this time?"

"Amber!" Rudy walked up just in time to hear Amber's comeback. "What's with you? Is criticizing Dorian going to make you feel better about losing?"

"Coach—"Amber protested.

"No," Rudy interrupted. He turned to face the other players. "You guys need to lighten up. All of you. This is *little league.* It's not life or death."

Zane sighed. It didn't matter anymore, anyway. He had been hoping to drop the news on his coach after the game, but this was definitely not the time. Rudy had already launched into his customary postgame speech. A cluster of waiting parents formed outside the dugout fence. Zane surveyed the group, disappointed once again. His mom was taking this too far. She had still not texted him back, even though Zane was trying to be nice.

Really sorry about the door. Are you at least coming to pick me up?

As the players started leaving, Rudy started looking at the scorebook with his assistant coaches, Ches and Vic. Zane waited it out for a few minutes before giving up and heading toward the street. He looked back at his coach one last time. Sure enough, still talking. Zane decided to send Rudy a text, even though he knew it was the cowardly thing to do.

He called his mom again.

No answer.

Blood rushed into Zane's cheeks. So, that's how it's gonna be? Zane no longer wanted to apologize. He wanted to yell even more.

CHAPTER 2

THE WALK HOME would take only fifteen minutes, but Zane didn't want to make the trip on foot. Clouds were forming, and that strange homeless man was back in the parking lot today. He thought of asking someone for a ride. Sammy? Ricky? He didn't really know any of them well enough. Zane's eyes darted back to his phone, convincing himself he may have missed something. Outside of a spam call from "Unknown" an hour earlier, he had squat.

He put his head down and began his trek.

"Hey, wait up."

Zane looked back to see Teddy stuffing his jersey inside his bag. He struggled with the zipper, then finally got it to close. The guy always seemed a bit tense.

"You walking, too?" Zane asked.

"Yeah." Teddy smiled. "I gotta go past Vine."

"Crocker and fifth," Zane said. The boys started out.

"Shorty's back," Teddy said. "Let's go that way."

Zane tried his best to sound cool. "He's just asking for money."

"That dude creeps me out. The way he's always looking at us. I don't know."

"I saw Amber say hi to him," Zane said.

"Doesn't mean I have to," Teddy said.

The short man with broad shoulders and no neck was carrying a white garbage bag stuffed with cans. He made eye contact with the boys and smiled. Something about that smile made all the players uneasy whenever they saw him. Teddy and Zane waited to see if he was going to approach.

"Sure you don't want to call your parents?" Zane asked.

"It's just my dad and me," Teddy said. "He wasn't feeling up to driving today."

Zane realized he had more in common with Teddy than he thought. Zane looked back. Shorty was gone. The boys resumed their walk. Zane was curious to know more about Teddy but also didn't want to pry.

"You okay?" Teddy asked.

"You mean the game?"

"Yeah."

"It's fine."

"I'd be upset, too," Teddy said. "Like those idiots would have even come close to making that catch? You just forgot the situation."

"I know. It's whatever. But it sucks having everyone blame you."

"That's kinda the reason I wanted to walk with you. That dropped ball—I shouldn't have let you take the blame on that. It was my fault. I owe you one."

"I should have called you off," Zane said. "I had it. No big deal."

"Well, it was to me," Teddy said.

Zane just stared ahead as the two walked on for a bit.

"You mad at me?" Teddy asked.

"Oh, I'm really not. It's just my… never mind."

"Uh, okay."

Zane looked at Teddy and shrugged his shoulders. "It's my mom. She totally ditched me today."

"What do you mean?"

"We had a fight. I lost my cool, but she was still supposed to come."

"What about your dad?" Teddy asked.

Zane paused for a second. He started to answer, then stopped, not sure what to say to a kid he didn't know that well.

Teddy picked up on the cue and changed the subject. "What was the fight about?"

"I slammed the door," Zane said proudly. "Many times. The knob busted right out. I grabbed my stuff and ran out of there. I thought she was going to say I was grounded, but I guess she knew it was her fault. She said she would meet me at Falcon. I told her 'don't bother.' But I didn't mean it."

"That explains the walk," Teddy said, starting to relax. "Why's it her fault?"

"She cares more about her job than me," Zane said. "This was our third move in four years. I'm the new guy on the team every season. When I brought it up again, she told me to 'suck it up.' After everything we had to go through. That's when I lost it."

"What's her job?" Teddy asked.

"That's the stupidest part. Data Analyst. Like you couldn't do that job anywhere. But she likes working for the government, so I get to move again and again. Now here we are in D.C." Zane knew it wasn't the full story about why they moved this time. It wasn't even close. But it was true about the other moves, and he didn't have the time or energy to break it all down.

"Government?" Teddy asked.

"Some division called the CRU. It stands for Cyber-security Reinforcement Unit. It's one of many, many departments inside the CIA complex in Langley," Zane said. "It sounds way cooler than it is."

"Your mom works in Langley? For reals?" They turned the corner.

"For real," Zane said, ignoring the extra "s" on "real." "Before this, she used to work at the NSA, and we lived just north of Baltimore. Anyways, she gets the honor of being one of the twenty thousand people that go to the George Bush Center for Intelligence to sit at a desk and stare at a screen all day."

"Well, it sounds pretty cool to me."

"You're definitely more impressed than me. But I didn't mean to unload all of that on you."

"I asked," Teddy said, stopping on the sidewalk. "Anyways, this is me. See ya tomorrow."

"See ya."

Teddy turned back. "Oh, and Zane."

"Yeah?"

"If you ever wanna tell me about your dad sometime, you can."

"Thanks," Zane said, smiling at Teddy. Then Zane started to go.

"Oh. And also—" Teddy said.

Zane turned back again.

"Don't let those guys get to you. Erik and Braxton are just mad at the world that they didn't make a travel team. And Dorian? Nobody knows what his problem is."

Zane was about to let Teddy know that Dorian, Braxton, and Erik were the furthest thing from his mind. But he saw the concern in Teddy's eyes.

"Thanks, man. I appreciate it."

"Somebody needed to stand up to that Dorian guy," Teddy said.

"Like Amber?"

Teddy smiled. "Yeah. She's something else."

Zane let out a quick laugh before stopping himself.

Teddy snapped out of his daydream. "I didn't mean it like that."

"All good. I won't say anything."

"Say anything about what?" Teddy asked.

"Exactly."

"I'm going home now," Teddy said.

The boys fist bumped. Zane watched Teddy head to his house, feeling like he had a friend for the first time since arriving in the Hillandale neighborhood a month and a half ago. The thought quickly turned bittersweet as he realized he wasn't being totally honest with Teddy.

As Zane rounded the corner to his street, he remembered how mad he was at his mom. What would he say? Should he come in mad? Apologetic? He was so lost in thought he almost walked past the huge, black SUV parked in his driveway. Just as Zane arrived, a tall, older man stepped out.

"Zane Clayborn?" he asked.

Zane Mitchell got that mistake a lot. His parents, Ryan and Mallory Clayborn, had given Zane his grandparents' last name as a way to honor them. Most adults assumed Zane's last name was Clayborn, as well. Zane sized up the stranger in his driveway and decided not to correct him. "Hi."

"Preston Burnett," the man said. He wore a light gray suit, a pink bowtie and a worried look. "From your mom's office. Remember?"

Zane had met a few of his mom's co-workers a month earlier but didn't remember Preston. No harm in being polite though. "Oh, yeah," he lied. "How's it going?" He walked past Preston and on to the front step. "I'll let my mom know you're here. She's inside."

"Actually," Preston said. "She's not."

CHAPTER 3

ALARM BELLS WENT off inside Zane's head. He cautiously turned back around to face the stranger and went over his options. Zane could try to quickly unlock the door and slip inside, but what if this guy was crazy and tried to push his way in at the exact moment Zane's back was turned? He considered running away from the house, but Preston was in between him and the street. Zane calmed his nerves and decided to play it cool, hoping this guy had a legit explanation. As a precaution, Zane angled his body sideways to make himself a smaller target. His dad was a dork but a street-smart dork that had taught him well.

"What do you mean?" he asked Preston. "Where is she? Is she okay?"

"Of course, of course," Preston said in a soothing voice. He took a step back. "Sorry, I didn't mean to scare you like that. She had to rush to work. She sent me. We have a bit of an emergency right now."

"On a Saturday?" Zane asked. "Why didn't she call me and tell me?" His mom kept weird hours but always kept Zane in the loop. No argument was about to change that.

"She did call," Preston said.

"That unknown number? It was during the game."

"That was the secure line," Preston said. "She doesn't have her phone. We can call her back in a minute and sort this all out."

"Sort *what* out?" Zane asked.

"Could we please go inside?" Preston asked.

Zane's feet didn't move. "Sorry, I don't know you." As Zane called his mom, he noticed the leatherbound government ID dangling from a silver chain around Preston's neck. The call went straight to voicemail this time.

Preston took another step back. "This is weird for me, too. I'll reach her for you from my phone, but it has to be a quick call on a secure line, and we can only call once. I need to explain a few things first, and I wanted to do that inside."

"What if I say no?"

"You might start to wonder when your mom is coming back."

"I can live with that," Zane said. "See ya." He turned to open the door as quickly as possible.

"Please! At least listen then. Our country is facing a serious threat right now."

Zane was holding his keys near the lock. He turned halfway back.

Preston looked around nervously to see if anyone was within earshot. His voice was quiet but firm. "There are very sensitive documents, saved on encrypted servers, that have suddenly come under attack. The hacker is on the ground here in D.C. If they can successfully hack in and copy these files, it puts many lives at risk."

"And what does this have to do with my mom?"

"Getting there," Preston said as he fidgeted with his tie. "The Cybersecurity Reinforcement Unit needs every hand on deck, so they called everybody in until this crisis is solved. She won't be leaving the building for a long time, even if she wanted to. She can't even access her phone. We're operating under extremely high security measures. I know this is a bit unusual, but that's how the CRU works. Your mom is serving our country."

"It sounds like you're keeping her hostage."

"Protecting the country is our chosen profession. We all want to help, regardless of any inconveniences. This is what we do. Everyone there has rooms to sleep in and everything they need. It's like a hotel. Every department within the CRU is helping with this one."

"She never had to do this when she worked inside the NSA," Zane challenged.

"This isn't the NSA."

"How long is all this going to take?" Zane asked.

"That's the million-dollar question. Sooner the better, but I'd be lying if I said I knew."

"Days?"

"Hopefully," Preston said. "Week at most."

"What about me?"

"I better let her tell you the plan. This is a unique situation. So, if it's all right with you, I'd like to get your mom on the phone, and we can all talk it through."

Zane looked through his front window into the living room. His mom had hung up the big, framed wedding photo that had moved with them from city to city. It brought them comfort to have Ryan's presence in their home. Their hair was ridiculous, but those were two of the biggest smiles Zane had ever seen on a pair of human beings. "You really need her to help save the country?"

"Well, there *is* actually another person we need even more," Preston said.

"Who's that?"

"You."

CHAPTER 4

"WHAT ARE YOU talking about?" Zane asked.

Preston motioned to the door.

"I have to talk to her first," Zane said.

A car drove down their street, and Preston eyed it carefully. After it turned, Preston dialed a number and hit speaker. "We can only talk once, and her voice will be warped," Preston said. "It might drop out some. Security filters. Can't take any chances."

When the call picked up, Preston spoke first. "Mallory, I have Zane on the phone. You're on speaker. We're on your front step. Can you tell him it's okay to let me in?"

"Hi, Zane," Mallory's deep, computer-altered voice said. *"Are you BEEP BEEEEEEEP?"* A distracting tone covered up the rest.

"Mom? Is that you?"

"Yes, sorry about scaring you like this. I tried to call. I gave Preston my keys since he'll be BEEP. He's okay to let in."

Zane looked at Preston, who held up the keys. Zane

saw his mom's shiny cat keychain reflect a glint of sunlight. "You mean you could have come in already?" Zane asked Preston.

"That would have really freaked you out," Preston said.

"Zane, it's all right," Mallory said. *"BEEP BEEP to talk."*

"Fine," Zane said. He turned and unlocked the door. He led the man inside their house on Crocker Street, in the Hillandale suburb of the nation's capital. Zane led Preston back to the kitchen table. They had a seat, and Preston placed the phone on the table between them. Zane hoped Preston hadn't noticed the bedroom door, a perfectly round hole where the doorknob had been just a few hours before.

There were some more beeps, and then Mallory's altered voice came back. *"Sorry I missed your game. BEEP BEEP BEEEEEP. BEEP they BEEP BEEEEEP wasn't enough time. I called BEEP BEEP you okay?"*

"Yeah, I guess," Zane said.

"Let's get to it," Preston said. "We only have a few minutes here, and the meter is running. Setting up another call would take me at least an hour and three clearance levels."

"Preston says you won't be coming home for days, maybe even a week?" Zane said. "Are you okay? And what does this have to do with me? You're not having Ms. Neely come down, are you?"

"Slow down," Mallory said. *"BEEP perfectly fine. I'm just doing my job. Preston is going to stay with you for a few days."*

Zane was floored. "Are you crazy? I don't know this guy. And I can stay on my own. I'll be a freshman in high school in a month."

"BEEP won't even know he's there," Mallory said.

"That's not entirely true," Preston said. "The whole reason I'm here is that I need you to help me. We need to work together on this."

"Sorry, but this is totally uncomfortable," Zane said. "It's not okay."

"You don't have any other family or friends to stay with," Preston said.

"I'll stay with Neely," Zane blurted out. "She can come. Baltimore's only an hour away." During the nineteen months they lived outside Baltimore, the strict, elderly Ms. Neely would stay with Zane whenever Mallory would go on work trips. Zane hated how she didn't let him go anywhere. Mallory was currently in the process of finding someone in Hillandale that could watch Zane for when the next work trip came in the Fall, but so far they had no one.

"She's unavailable," Mallory said.

"Mom!"

Preston spoke up. "This is what your mom thought was best, considering what the CRU is about to ask you to do."

"That's what nobody has told me yet," Zane said.

"Zane, what I am about to tell you is classified," Preston said. "If you repeat this to anyone, the United States government could come after you. I'm telling you this because I feel it's absolutely necessary. Do you understand?"

"Yes."

Preston gave him a serious look, then continued. "The reason for all of this is a new cyberattack. Somebody has found a weakness in our system and figured out a way to hack in and steal the O-I-L."

"They want to steal *oil?*" Zane asked.

"It stands for Operative Identity List," Preston said. "It lists every undercover operative the U.S. has."

"We're talking about spies?" Zane asked.

"Yes," Preston said. "The OIL has three separate files. Current codenames, actual identities, and a decoder key that allows you to match up the first two lists. Losing the three OIL files would endanger the lives of hundreds and hundreds of operatives. And these operatives are all directly responsible for stopping terrorist attacks. If they are killed or captured, hundreds of thousands of people could be next."

Zane's cell phone started ringing. He quickly silenced it.

"Sorry," Zane said. "I still don't see—"

"The attack is coming from your field, kid." Preston interrupted.

"Falcon Field? I thought cyberattacks came through the internet."

"They do," Preston said. "The hacker can usually be anywhere in the world. Not this time." Preston took out a sleek black iPad and powered it on. He tapped a few times and showed Zane a map of Washington, D.C. He tapped on a paint tool, then used his finger to draw a circle around two buildings. "These are the two most important buildings we have in the intelligence community. Here in Langley, and thirty miles northeast at the National Security Agency in Fort Meade." He drew a line between the two circles and continued. "There is a wireless information link that runs between those two buildings. We call it the Link. It is completely secure to hackers from all over the world. But somebody figured out that if you set up your equipment in an exact, magic spot halfway between the two buildings, there is a way to trick the defense system. You couldn't do it from anywhere else but this exact spot, give or take one hundred feet." Preston put his finger back on the screen. He made another circle in the Hillandale suburb, right around Falcon Field. "There."

"Falcon Field is the magic spot?" Zane asked.

"The weak spot. The hacker is setting up there, tricking the system into thinking this is the end of the information link." He tapped his finger on the new circle. "The CRU needs to investigate."

"Does that make sense, Zane?" his mom chimed in from the speaker. *"I know this is a lot… to take in."*

"What do you need me for?" Zane asked. "Why don't you guys just go to the field and stay there until you catch the hacker?"

"The attacks have been happening in roughly hour-and-a-half bursts," Preston said. "There have been three, all from Diamond One. It started six days ago. Sunday from four p.m. to five thirty p.m. Then it happened again Wednesday from five p.m. to six thirty p.m. And today from three until just about twenty minutes ago. Do you recognize those times?"

"Wait, are those—"

"Yes," Preston said. "The attacks have happened during the Renegades' last three games. We want to get close to investigate, but we can't get on the field."

"Why not?" Zane asked.

"The problem is that we cannot let this enemy spy know we're on to them yet," Preston said. "I take pride in completing my assignments on my own, but to get what I need, I need to physically be standing next to their hidden piece of equipment, which is in the middle of the field. And we assume they have surveillance cameras watching the field twenty-four seven. If they saw me out there, they'd bolt. We really have to know who's doing this and why. It will take them a while to steal the codename file and the identity file, and they also need the decoder key. So, we feel we have time to gather intel on the culprit before the risk gets too great. In other words, we can't scare them off yet. We really want to see what they get and who they're dealing with. But again, if the hacker thinks somebody is on to them, the game's over, and they vanish."

"Is that why you don't just bulldoze the whole field?" Zane asked.

"Exactly. We don't actually want you to stop the attack yet. At this point, we just want you to find this device and get information."

"And why is it happening only during my games?" Zane asked. "Some spy is coming to Falcon Field during my games and doing his thing while we play?"

"No," Preston said. "The attacks are coming from somewhere between the base lines. We've pinpointed the location down to a very small radius. The spy has to be—"

"Who?" Zane demanded.

"One of your teammates. We just don't know which one yet."

"You're joking," Zane said.

"Dead serious. Whoever is doing this has been on the field during those exact times. We checked out your coaches: Chester Logan, Victor Perez, Paul Rudella. They've been ruled out. "

"Rudy's name is Paul?"

"Yes. Clean. The umpires change every game. We know it's a player carrying out this mission. It's the only explanation. And I need you to help me figure out who it is and what they've got."

Zane stood up. "Hold on. You're saying one of my fourteen-year-old teammates is actually a dangerous spy?"

"Yes, we're trying to figure out why. As far as the 'how,' I'm guessing they've been laying the groundwork for this all season and began the cyberattack last week. It's almost certainly a player that is new on the team this year, or joined midseason. Did anybody just join up?"

"Besides me? No."

"Try to figure out who's new to the team this year and doesn't have a normal backstory," Preston said. "That's your starting point. Maybe the family situation seems off. If this spy has a 'parent' show up, that parent would also have to be a fake. Figure out who doesn't belong."

"Is the cyberattack coming from another country?" Zane asked, thinking of his teammates who may be new in the U.S.

"It could be any of your teammates, regardless of their nationality. Oh, and of course we're also assuming it has to be someone who was there each of the past three games."

"And you're sure about all this?" Zane asked again.

"I wouldn't be here if I wasn't. Have you seen any computer equipment on the field or in the dugout?"

Zane thought for a second. "No, sorry."

"This is why we need you," Mallory said through the static on the phone.

"The Cybersecurity Reinforcement Unit is a special appointment that has certain freedoms," Preston said. "In other words, I can pretty much do what I need to do to investigate cyberattacks and act in our best interest. In this case, that… 'flexibility' I'll call it… means asking a teenager for a few favors during his ball game."

"So, you want me to figure out who it is—without letting them know?" Zane asked.

"Nobody can know," Preston said. "Not even your coaches. If they knew, they might act differently and tip our hand. If the spy found out, they would run and not hesitate to use deadly force. So, play it cool. All we need you to do is help *identify* the hacker and *gather* information. We'll handle the hard stuff at the right time."

"How do you know I'm not the spy?" Zane asked.

"We know your mom, and we know you," Preston said. "It's everybody else that is unknown. And we have to act fast."

Zane maintained steady eye contact with Preston. "But if one of my teammates is dangerous, it's not safe to go back. The other kids shouldn't be there either."

"Listen," Preston said. "The bigger danger is letting this person slip away without us knowing what's going on. You have to think of the big picture."

"I don't think I can do this," Zane said.

"There's nobody else," Preston said. "If we send in somebody new, or an adult, the hacker will suspect something is off. You are already on the team. All your games are on Diamond One. It is the perfect cover. Get to know your teammates better. Watch them carefully. We can show you what else you'll need to do. The hacker won't see this coming."

"I'd be a spy, spying on another spy," Zane said. "If I could find out whoever the spy is."

"Zane," Mallory said from the phone. *"Preston has assured us there will be undercover BEEP during BEEP."*

Preston nodded. "The CRU will protect you. We're more than just Data Analysts. We have many departments on our team, including Federal Agents that are as highly trained and capable as they come."

Zane twisted his blue baseball cap backward, then forward again.

"Zane, you can do this" his mom said. *"You have to."*

Zane's phone buzzed again. This time a text message. Zane gave it a quick glance before looking back at Preston. "So, you really think one of my teammates is trying to get this list that will get a bunch of people killed?"

"I don't think it, I know it," Preston said. "I have classified information that leaves no doubt. I also have no doubt that you're the perfect person in the perfect situation to help your country."

Zane took a breath. "I would love to help you. But, uh... I can't."

Preston's mouth opened wide.

Zane heard his mom say, *"What?"*

Zane looked at his phone again. "I kind of just quit the team."

CHAPTER 5

"YOU'VE GOT TO be kidding," Preston said.

"I'm not," Zane said. "Sorry."

"You can't quit," his mom said.

"What do you mean 'kind of'?'" Preston asked.

"I texted Rudy, 'It's best if I leave the team. It's not working out.' That was him calling me back. And texting."

"I thought you loved BEEP." His mom's distorted voice sounded unusually calm.

"In reality, a lot of my teammates kinda suck. It's not my idea of fun to have Dorian call me a loser and have people laugh. I can't relax, we never win, and we're probably moving again anyways. What's the point?"

"I could think of a few pretty good points for you to keep playing," Preston said. "Do you understand the gravity of the situation here?"

Zane felt his face getting hot. "This is crazy. All of a sudden you show up talking about 'crews' and 'oils,' my mom's gone, you want to stay with me, and I'm supposed to save the world by finding out which one of my jerk teammates is actually a dangerous spy?"

"You have to do what Preston says," Mallory said.

"Are you nervous?" Preston asked.

"Absolutely. I guess I don't understand why you can't do it yourself. You're the professionals. Stop the hacker's device from the stands. Use computers. You could still do it without them knowing."

"We've tried," Preston said, "but we can't figure out how to do it remotely. We have a way to look at the spy's receiver and see what they've stolen, but we need to basically stand on the receiver to do it. And as I said, these people are probably watching the field twenty-four seven, so we have to get this done discreetly during the normal course of the game. It's the best way. We can't get as close as you without raising suspicion. You give us the element of surprise, and we can't lose that. Doing it this way saves lives, plain and simple. Asking for your help feels weird, but it's the best course of action. And we really aren't asking you to do that much."

"Mom, I don't feel okay with him staying here."

"He's a good man trying to complete an assignment," Mallory said. *"It only makes sense. You help him with this BEEP eye on you for a few days."*

"I have something else for you," Preston said. He reached into his suit pocket and took out a stack of credit cards wrapped in a rubber band. "Ten prepaid, two hundred dollar VISA gift cards. For whatever expenses we have while your mom's gone. It's way more than we'll need, but they give these to me to use at my discretion. Personally, I don't need them. You can be in charge of the cards. Eat like a king the next few days, buy whatever, I don't care. Keep the rest once this is all over with."

Zane couldn't believe what he was looking at. Helping out the Cybersecurity Reinforcement Unit suddenly didn't sound so unreasonable.

"Mom?"

Mallory's distorted voice chimed in from the speaker. *"I guess it's your lucky day. Preston, are you sleeping in the guest room?"*

"Yes. And when we're not doing the mission, I'll stay out of Zane's way, or be at work."

Zane read the latest text. Rudy was ticked. *"Are you seriously quitting? And you aren't answering? Fine."*

"Look," Preston said. "Each time your team takes the field, that spy moves one step closer to putting undercover American agents in extreme danger. Are you going to help? Or will you stand around and do nothing?"

Zane looked at Preston, and their eyes met. Neither one looked away. It was clear this man was not leaving until he heard what he wanted. Zane could at least play along for now. He reached out and took the stack of cards. He ran his thumb over the bumpy account numbers on the top. "Specifically speaking, what do you need me to do?"

Preston smiled. "Two things. First, we have to find the receiver they are using."

"Without them knowing, right?" Zane asked.

Preston nodded. "Our spy is using a small receiver device to 'receive' the OIL files he is stealing from the Link. The receiver is sucking in the signal, trying to pick off the files it wants. It's hidden somewhere in the middle of Falcon Field. It is the size of a deck of cards. I'll show you how to find it. Your mission is to secretly copy the files that have been stolen. Copy the intercepted files."

"Okaaayyy," Zane said. "And you're sure I can't just sneak in later today after Falcon Field clears out? No one'll be around."

"Enemy surveillance, remember?" Preston said. "They'd know we are on to them. That's the reason we need you. You have to locate the receiver within the normal confines of the game—without arousing suspicion. And then there's that *other* thing we need done."

"Figure out which one of my teammates is working against the United States government. You realize these kids barely talk to me? Some of them hate me. Not to mention, I'm not a spy. I'm just a kid."

"You can do this," Mallory said.

"And how exactly do you expect me to pull this off?" Zane asked.

"For starters," Preston said, "call back that coach of yours and ask him to let you back on the team."

CHAPTER 6

MONDAY FINALLY CAME. Preston had been a man of his word and barely spoke to Zane over the weekend. He had been either in the guest room, door shut, or at work the entire time. But now that game day was here, Preston spent the morning going over everything again in detail with Zane. T*wice. Preston wished him luck, and then Zane was on his way.

For the first time since joining the Renegades, he got to Falcon Field early. It was a beautiful day. The four fields that made up the complex were coming alive in advance of the first wave of games. Lines were chalked, home plates freshly dusted, and the scoreboards were powered on, flashing zeroes. The grass looked as green as it had all summer, and some early-arrivers from each team were already enjoying the space. A few adults busied themselves in the centrally-located concession stand. Zane's stomach growled as he walked past the smell of fresh kettle corn being bagged up. Usually, his mom made him a breakfast burrito the morning before a game. Since Zane was too anxious to use the kitchen, he'd opted to shove a measly granola bar in his mouth. Not having his mom's cooking was going to be tough.

He wore his trusty baseball backpack, with his favorite two bats on each side. Normally, each bat had an upside down cleat on it, but Zane needed to have his new cleats securely zipped inside his bag. He saw his coaches, Rudy, Ches, and Vic, already by the dugout. Ches and Vic's sons, teammates Sammy and Mateo, were running around being silly. Zane figured he could rule those two players out but still wasn't ready to approach them. He quickly turned right and headed for the opposite field. There was an additional bathroom building located between the opposite parking lot and entrance. He tried to walk as casually as possible. It wasn't easy. He finally got to the small, brick bathroom facility and was relieved to see it was empty. He slipped inside and was disappointed to find the door wouldn't lock.

He looked at himself in the mirror. *Breathe, buddy.* He went inside a stall and locked that door. He reached into his back pocket and took out the special coin his dad had given him on what proved to be the last time Zane would ever see him. The coin had a strange shape on each side. His dad had simply said it was for good luck and to hang on to it. Zane kept it with him ever since. He put it back in his pocket and got to work. He unzipped his backpack and took out his left cleat. He stared at the bottom of the shoe in amazement. Inside his front spike was something Preston called "a digital proximity sensor." Preston had programmed it to detect the spy's hidden receiver. The closer it was to its target, the faster it would signal to his earpiece.

He tapped his finger against the edge of another spike. Inside was a tiny computer chip that would copy whatever files were on the receiver on to a removable micro SD card. All of it was completely covered by the rubber of the spikes. He wondered how much the U.S. government spent on his cleats.

He looked at his belt. Incredibly, it looked like just a belt. He ran his thumb up and down the smooth outside edge of the buckle and heard the volume in his earpiece go higher and lower. He heard a hiss. Barely. He touched his buckle again and raised it back to full volume. The hissing noise came back. He wanted to hear at least one beep to see how loud it would be.

Nothing but static.

And the beating of his heart, sounding like it would explode through his jersey.

He took off his crocs and put them in his bag. He laced up his cleats, left the stall, and washed his hands, partly from habit, partly for show. He looked at the mirror again and examined his left ear. His wavy, light brown hair was just long enough to conceal the earpiece. Zane thanked himself for ignoring his mom's pleas to cut it and pulled the hair back to get a look. The earpiece was tiny and blended in flawlessly. It made him relax a little, especially when he let his hair fall back in place and straightened his cap. He took one last look into his own brown eyes, wondering if he was really going through with this.

Zane walked along the outfield fence, toward Diamond One. From a distance he could still immediately spot Rudy's round upper body and tucked T-shirt. Zane's coach had said he wanted to talk in person before warmups. Some more Renegades had arrived and were playing catch in left field. How could one of these kids possibly be a danger to our country? Did he even really know them?

"Hey," Amber said. "I heard you were quitting?"

"How'd you hear that?" Zane asked.

"Coaches were talking."

"Nope." Zane patted his uniform.

Dorian and Erik walked past, each wearing their baseball sunglasses.

"Shoot," Erik said. "I'm pitching today and thought for a second I'd have some players on defense that knew what to do."

Dorian laughed.

Zane was about to say something but bit his lip and simply watched the boys strut past.

"Dopes," Amber said. "You can't quit, though."

"Why's that?"

"Because I need someone out here worse than me." Amber smiled.

"Ouch." Zane smiled back. He kept walking. Amber had dark wavy hair, soft green eyes, and a muscular build. She may have been the shortest player on the team, but you could spot her confidence a mile away. She acted like she belonged. He could see why Teddy had eyes for her.

"Zane!" called Rudy from the dugout. His coach was walking out to left field to meet him. "There you are. Let's take a walk."

As Zane waited for his coach, he fidgeted with his belt. Still no beep to let him know he was close to the receiver.

"I see you came dressed to play," Rudy said as he got out to Zane in left field.

"I didn't mean it, coach."

"Mean what? We've barely talked. If there was a problem, why didn't you come to me? And why text me something so important?"

"I should've called," Zane said. "I'm sorry."

"Were you avoiding me?"

"I'm not fitting in. I thought things would get worse if you got involved."

"Son, do you realize over half the kids on this team moved here within the past year or two?"

"I didn't know that," Zane said.

Rudy started walking back toward the dugout and motioned with his head for Zane to follow. "Government town like this?" Rudy said. "Families are coming in and out all the time. You need to cut yourself some slack. Being new isn't easy, but everybody goes through it. Especially here. The main thing is you get to play the game you love."

BEEP!

Zane spun around to see if he could see the receiver anywhere.

"Are you mocking me?" Rudy asked.

"No, no. I thought I heard… sorry. I wasn't making a face at you, I swear."

Rudy looked dissatisfied. "To be honest, Zane Mitchell, I am not convinced the other kids are the problem. You haven't been the easiest guy to be around."

Zane knew his coach would cut him some slack if he only knew about the accident three years earlier. But

Zane kept it in. "I wanna play. It's been hard. I have some things going on right now. But I'll have a better attitude."

BEEP! BEEP!

The proximity sensor in his cleats was detecting the hidden receiver, causing his earpiece to beep. The noises were coming in more frequently as they walked down the third base line, approaching the dugout. Zane did his best to appear engaged in the conversation. He wondered if his cleats would actually make the download when the moment came. He might even be able to complete his mission in one day.

"So, do you think you want to give this another shot?" Rudy asked.

BEEP! BEEP! BEEP!

Zane held up his glove. "Absolutely,"

"Me, too," Rudy said. "As soon as you sit out today's game as punishment, then you're back on the team."

CHAPTER 7

"COACH, I REALLY would like to play today," Zane said.

"A few days ago you were ready to quit," Rudy said. "I'm happy you want to be back with us. But I talked to Ches and Vic. There has to be some kind of penalty. It's one game."

"I know I was letting my team down if I quit. That's why I came back. I want to win. I'm dressed and ready to go. If I sit, what's the point?"

"The point is that you'll realize how lucky we are to have this sport and this chance to come out and play. Plus you learn the importance of communicating with people in person instead of hiding behind a phone."

Zane heard the beeping increase. "I guess you're right. I understand."

"Be a good teammate today, and we'll have you back in the lineup for the next game."

"Okay." Zane turned toward the field, ready to find the receiver.

"Bench is that way," Rudy said, pointing to the third base dugout.

"Could I at least warm up with the guys?" Zane asked.

"Not today."

BEEP! BEEP! BEEP! BEEP!

Zane thought about ignoring his coach and wandering around until he found the receiver. He looked back at Rudy, staring right at him, waiting for him to serve his punishment. If he disobeyed his coach, he doubted he'd ever get another chance.

"But coach—"

"Enough!" Rudy put his hands on his hips. "If you have a good attitude today, you'll be back on the field tomorrow for that makeup game against the Panthers. This conversation is over."

"'Kay." Zane walked past third base and could feel Rudy watching him. He heard the beeping intensify even more. Once the beeping turned into a steady tone, he'd be in range. He would then need to stand still for twenty seconds, allowing his cleats to download whatever files the receiver had stolen. As he moved further past third base, the beeping slowed. He slowed his walk but had to keep moving past as his teammates warmed up.

"What was that all about?" Braxton asked with a glint in his eye.

"Nothing," Zane said. He wasn't about to give Braxton the same chance that Erik had to say something snarky. Zane entered the dugout and took a seat. The beeping slowed even more. As the rest of his teammates arrived, a sense of panic crept up his chest. Who was he looking for? What if they spotted him first?

"Hey, Z!" Teddy said. "Stop daydreaming and come warm up."

It couldn't be Teddy. Could it?

"Sorry. Coach says I have to sit out the game. Can't even warm up."

"For reals?" Teddy asked.

"For real," Zane said, once again ignoring Teddy's go-to expression.

"Why?"

"I texted Rudy that I wanted to quit. But I didn't really mean it. Anyways, he didn't like how I handled it, so here I am."

Teddy's smile disappeared. "You were quitting?"

Zane could see Teddy felt betrayed. And even though Teddy could be the spy, Zane felt bad.

"Nah," Zane said. "I just didn't want to keep trying. It's hard to explain. But I thought about it and decided to come back."

"I get it," Teddy said. "More than you realize."

"You do?"

"Yeah, man. I felt like that at first, too. Still do sometimes. But once in a while, there's that moment out here that makes all the crap worth it."

"Hope so."

"Well, I'm glad you didn't quit," Teddy said.

"Thanks," Zane said. "You'll have me back after today's game."

"Maybe we'll have you today also."

"What do you mean?"

"I heard the Atwaters are both at the Nats game. If you're out, too, Rudy's down to nine players."

Vic's son, Mateo Perez, walked in the dugout. "Weren't you going to the Nats today also?"

"I missed one of our games last week, so my dad says I should play today," Teddy said. "Point is, Zane, you're the only sub. You never know."

Outfielder Ricky Martinez strolled into the dugout next, plopped down his bat bag, and made a big pop with his bubble gum. Catcher Sammy Logan was right behind him. They were about to head back out to the field. Zane was about to lose his chance to make some small talk.

"Uh, hey guys," Zane said.

Ricky was startled at Zane's rare greeting. "Oh, hey. Sorry, you have to sit."

Sammy smeared some eye black on his cheeks. "Yeah, sucks. Why'd he shelve you?"

"For almost quitting," Zane said. "Makes perfect sense, right?"

"Bro, you aren't exactly the first guy Rudy has made an example of," Ricky said, popping an even bigger bubble than before.

"It's a respect thing," Sammy said. "You guys know that he has an entire series of motivational speeches saved on a flash drive on his key chain?"

"A flash drive?" Mateo asked.

"Yeah, like a little stick you can save files on and plug into a computer," Sammy said. "They used to be a thing."

"Like a VCR," Mateo said.

"He told me about it one time," Sammy said. "Says he wants it near him at all times just in case he needs the inspiration."

"That's Rudy for ya," Ricky said. "At least he cares."

"Say, how many years have you guys been on this team?" Zane asked. This was the most he had chatted with these guys all season. He joined in conversations here and there but never really initiated anything.

"First year," Ricky said between smacks of his Bubblicious. "Moved from Philly in January."

"Fourth," Sammy said. "Mateo and I are the last ones left from our sixth-grade championship team."

"Nobody cares," Mateo said.

Zane was paying close attention. He could safely say Sammy and Mateo were not suspects. Not only were their dads assistant coaches, but their families had both lived here for years.

"First year, too," Teddy said.

"I never realized how many new guys we had," Zane said. "Who else?"

"Only half the team," Sammy said. "You, Teddy, Dorian, Ricky, Braxton, and Erik. One more, but I can't think of it."

"Amber," Zane said.

Ricky whacked Teddy in the butt with his glove. "Oh yeah, Amberrrrr."

Sammy started making out with his catcher's mitt. Mateo and Ricky started cracking up.

Teddy's cheeks turned bright red. "Are you done? She's gonna see you. She's gonna see you any second."

"Okay, leave him alone," Ricky said. "Teddy's already got a girlfriend. She lives in Canada."

Zane could tell Teddy was taking it in good fun, so he laughed along. The mood stiffened up as soon as Erik and Braxton returned to the dugout from their warmup.

"What?" Erik asked, eager to get in on the tail end of the joke.

"Nothing," Sammy said. "Let's toss, RickMart." Sammy and Ricky headed out, followed by Mateo and Teddy. Zane sat on the bench and thought. Preston's going theory was the hacker had to be someone new to the team this year, joining up after discovering the weakness in the Link.

Zane repeated the names to himself. *Dorian, Ricky, Braxton, Erik, Amber, Teddy. Dorian, Ricky, Braxton, Erik, Amber, Teddy. Dorian....*

A few minutes passed before Rudy called everyone in from the field. "All right, listen up. We're in the field first. Few changes from last time. Ricky, you take center for Z. Mateo, take third for Amber. Amber, go to left. Dorian's covering first, while Erik pitches."

It dawned on Zane that a different kid had played third each of the past three games. Rudy could not find anyone that could handle the position.

The Renegades finished their final pregame warmup. Zane sat on the bench with the coaches. Zane felt his belt buckle again, raising the volume to max. His earpiece beeped but only once every thirty seconds. He had to get to third base and find the receiver, but how? He imagined running out there and standing on the bag. Everyone on the team would think he was crazy, except the spy, who would then know what he was up to. Zane was in no rush to reveal himself to his unknown target. If he was going to get to third and stand for twenty seconds, he had to make it look as natural as possible.

If one of these kids was a spy, what about their parents? Were they here? Preston said that person or persons would be in on it as well, but there were a lot of things Preston didn't fully explain. Up to this point, Zane had spent his time on this team trying to blend in and made hardly any attempt to get to know his fellow Renegades, let alone their parents.

And here he was, stuck in a cage, wondering which one of his teammates carried a deadly secret.

Dorian, Ricky, Braxton, Erik, Amber, Teddy.

CHAPTER 8

ERIK WALKED THE first batter. The next batter hit a screamer right to Dorian, who simply caught it and stepped on first for a double play.

"Yes!" Erik yelled.

The rest of the team chirped in with "attaboys" and calls of "that's two!"

Zane kept his eyes glued to Dorian. The big, surly teenager made circles in the dirt with his cleats and tugged on his hat.

Was this his regular motion in between pitches, or a way to activate the illegal hacking device?

Zane looked over to shortstop and saw Braxton kicking his cleat into the dirt by second base. Zane tugged down on the bill of his cap. This was going to drive him crazy. His chest felt tighter than ever. Why did he ever say he would help?

The next batter flied out to Ricky, and the team jogged off the field. Ricky stepped on the third base bag on the way to the dugout. Zane suppressed another shot of anxiety and tucked the info away.

Dorian spoke so the whole team could hear. "Hey Rick, glad to see you know how to count to three!"

Some of the guys laughed. Zane clenched his fists and pretended he didn't hear the insult. He was about to attempt another round of small talk with these guys. Creating tension would not help his cause.

Amber walked over to Zane. "Braxton and Erik giving you crap still?"

"Mainly Dorian," Zane said. "But whatever."

"They're threatened by you."

"That's funny."

"No, you're a better player, and a better dude, but they'd already set up their alpha male act by the time you arrived."

She took off her hat, revealing a dark pony tail that had been tucked away. She rummaged through the bag and pulled out her helmet with a smile. Zane had to remind himself he was studying her as a potential spy, not checking her out.

"Some guys just aren't worth the time," Zane said. "I'm more likely to speak up when they mess with somebody else."

"Zane Mitchell, baseball hero," Amber said in a damsel-in-distress voice.

"I just don't need to make a thing out of it right now, that's all."

"Well, it's different for me. They just pretend I'm not there. Kinda like the rest of you guys."

"Hey, cooties are serious," Zane said.

"Dead serious," Amber replied, not missing a beat.

POP!

Everybody was staring at the other team's pitcher warming up before his first inning.

"No way that guy's fourteen," Mateo said.

"He skipped the mustache stage," Sammy said. "I think he's going straight for the goatee."

"I saw his wife and kids in the stands, watching," Ricky added.

"Who is that?" Zane asked. The pitches were faster than he had ever seen a kid throw.

"Nate Moosen," Sammy said. "They call him 'Moose.'"

Moose was tall like Zane but much broader in the chest and hips. His arms were enormous.

"Heard he beaned his own little brother last week in a tee-ball game," Ricky said.

"Well, *I* heard he smoked a cigarette in the dugout," Sammy said.

"You guys are idiots," Erik said.

Sammy grabbed his bat and practiced his stance. "All I'm saying is I wouldn't want to be on that guy's bad side."

Zane saw how distracted everyone was. He moved to the end of the dugout again, as close to third as he could get. The beeping got quicker.

Braxton was up first for the Renegades, but Moose blew three fastballs right past him.

"Mooooooooose!" yelled the Bombers' dugout. Braxton shook his head as he made the walk of shame back to his seat.

Ricky was up next and swung early. He made solid contact, sending a foul ball sailing over the Renegades' dugout on the third base side.

Zane hopped up. "Got it." He ran out of there before Rudy had the chance to stop him.

Zane heard two quick beeps and paused outside the fence near third base. He thought for a moment, then decided to keep jogging out toward the parking lot and track down the ball. Preston's orders were stressing him out. He thought about how easy it would be to not really try but tell the CRU man he did his best and it just wasn't possible. Surely Preston could figure out another way. Zane even pinpointed the location for him. That had to be enough.

The foul ball settled on the path between diamonds. When Zane got to it, he passed a young mother pushing a stroller. He looked back to the other side of the parking lot and saw a grandfather walking with his grandkids, covered in ice cream and enjoying a picture-perfect day. Zane thought back to Preston's speech about terrorists and imagined a bomb going off, fire raining from the sky. Zane felt chills go down his spine. He knew what his dad would want. Zane walked back to Diamond One, ball in hand.

Zane was mulling it over as he walked through the gate in the left field corner. He heard some "oohing" and laughing from the field but couldn't tell what he had missed. He ran along the inside of the fence toward the dugout. When he got to the edge of the dugout near third, he heard the beeping intensify.

"*Ball!*" the umpire called out upon seeing Zane.

"Here goes nothing," he told himself. Zane tossed the ball to the home plate ump, then purposely tripped on his own feet and laid on the ground.

BEEP! BEEP! BEEP!

Everybody laughed. Everybody except Moose, who turned fire engine red.

"You think you're funny?" he shouted from the mound.

"Zane, quit messing around," Rudy said.

BEEP! BEEP! BEEP! BEEP!

Zane got up slowly, waiting for the beeps to turn into a tone.

"Zane!" Rudy snapped again.

"I'm okay," Zane said. He wanted to wait for the swoosh, but everyone was staring at him. He gave up and headed into the dugout. The beeps slowed down. How close had he been to twenty seconds?

"Dude," Sammy said, eyes wide. "That takes some serious stones to make fun of him like that."

"It was funny though," Ricky said.

"What are you guys talking about?" Zane asked.

"You falling," Ricky said. "Duh."

"What do you mean? I slipped."

"You didn't see what happened to Moose?" Ricky asked.

"No, what?" Zane said.

"Ahhhh," Ricky said. "You must've missed it when you got the foul ball. Moose threw a pitch so hard he fell and face-planted on the mound. He ate serious dirt. It was great. We cracked up, and he got all mad. Right when we settled down, and I mean right as it ended, you came in and made fun of him."

"I wasn't making fun of him," Zane said. "I didn't even know he fell!"

"That's not what he thinks," Sammy said.

"Quit stressing him out," Mateo said. "What's Moose gonna do, anyways?"

Moose dominated the game with his pitching until the fifth inning, when he walked two, and Sammy came through with a line drive double. Erik, meanwhile, was pitching his best game of the season for the Renegades, who were benefiting from solid defense and had a surprising 3-1 lead going into the top of the seventh. That's when things started to get dicey. Cedric took over for Erik and got in a jam. Cedric tried to pick off a runner at third but threw it into the dirt. The ball went rolling, and two runs scored to tie it at 3-3. Then, a grounder bounced right through Mateo's legs at third, allowing the Bombers to go up 4-3. There were two outs.

The next batter hit a fly ball to right center. This time, Teddy ran with a purpose. His voice was assertive. "I got it!"

Teddy made a nice running catch to end the inning. Everybody cheered. As Teddy came out of his run, he made a face like he just drank spoiled milk. He reached back and grabbed his left hamstring. He winced in pain and limped all the way to the dugout.

"You okay?" Yuri asked.

"I don't think so," Teddy said.

"Teddy Rempke!" Rudy said. "What's up?"

"It feels like the worst cramp ever. Could I have torn it?"

"You wouldn't be standing here talking to us if you tore it," Coach Ches said. "Have a seat and stretch it out."

The Renegades were down a run and down to their final inning. Yuri started the bottom of the seventh by striking out. Amber followed that with her first hit in her last two games. They were in business. If somebody could drive her in, the Renegades would tie the score. Mateo was up, and Teddy was on deck.

"Coach, I can't even stand," Teddy said. "Something's messed up."

All at once, Zane felt everybody on the team whip their heads around and stare at him. Then back at Rudy.

Rudy said nothing.

"Strike three!" the umpire shouted. Mateo had stood there watching a called third strike.

Mateo clenched his bat and muttered, *"Ciego."*

"What'd that mean?" Sammy asked back in the dugout.

"Blind," Mateo told his teammates. "Let's hope the ump doesn't speak Spanish."

The guys let out a quick laugh before getting serious. The Renegades were down to their final out, and there was a problem.

"Coach?" Zane said. He held up his batting helmet. His batting gloves were on.

The umpire straightened up and looked over at the Renegades dugout. *"Batter up!"*

Zane gave Rudy a respectful look as he waited for the coach to put him in. Rudy turned from Zane to look over at his assistants coaching the bases. Ches had a blank stare, and Vic simply gave a noncommittal shrug. Rudy then looked at the lineup card hanging on the inside of the dugout fence.

He was lost in thought.

Teddy couldn't bat. If they skipped his turn in the order, the other manager could protest, and it would be ruled an out. Game over. If the Renegades put in a pinch hitter, the game wouldn't miss a beat. Rudy was old school. He was a man of his word and was intent on disciplining Zane. On the other hand, he knew it would be unfair to the whole team to basically forfeit the game over this. Zane continued to stare at Rudy with a hopeful expression.

The ump spoke up again. "Rudy, what's the holdup?"

CHAPTER 9

"ALL RIGHT, Z," Rudy said. "Make something happen."

His teammates all started to hoot and holler.

"Let's go, Zane!"

"Yeahhhhh Zaner!"

"Z-Bar time! Yip yip!"

Zane popped on his helmet. He patted his back pocket to make sure his lucky coin was still there. He slid his Easton Crusher out from his bag and wrapped his fingers around the grip. It felt good. His teammates were slapping him on the helmet as he emerged from the dugout.

"Come on, now!"

"Be a hero!"

"You got this now!"

He took a slow breath in and puffed it out. Zane had not felt this alive all season. Suddenly, all that mattered was him driving in the tying run. He stared at Moose as he walked to the left side of the batter's box. He took two quick practice swings and focused. Then, he heard it.

BEEP!

It all came back. Preston, his mom, the traitor posing as one of his teammates. He glanced toward third. He needed a triple. The rarest hit in baseball.

"Be patient," Coach Vic called from third. "We need a runner!"

Moose's first pitch looked way inside. Zane jerked his hips back, but the umpire called out, *"Strike!"*

Zane couldn't believe it. *"Ciego."*

"That's okay," Rudy said. "Wait for a good one."

Zane decided he couldn't let the umpire decide his fate. He would swing if the ball was anywhere in the right time zone. And he was swinging big. He didn't want to take the chance of getting only a single, then having the game end on the next batter.

BEEP!

BEEP! BEEP!

Zane looked at third, and then stepped in the batter's box. Then, he looked back at Moose and noticed a slight smile at the corner of the pitcher's mouth as he began his windup.

It was the fastest pitch Zane had ever seen—and it was coming right at his face! Zane tried to duck, but he wasn't quick enough. The ball hit him on the top of the helmet and ricocheted straight up in the air.

Zane slumped to the ground and took off his helmet. He put his hands on his head. It felt like a gong was going off inside his brain. The crowd gasped. Rudy rushed over to Zane.

The umpire scowled at Moose. "You're gone!" he yelled at the big pitcher. "That was intentional!"

Moose snorted. "It was an accident. It slipped."

"It was retaliation. I saw what happened earlier. Coach, get your pitcher out of here."

The Bombers coach, Nick Moosen, walked over with his hand up. "Now hold up. My son wouldn't do that."

"It's fine, who cares," Moose said, smiling ever so slightly as he strutted off the field.

"Are you okay?" Rudy asked Zane.

The words sounded like they were underwater, like someone had put a big, metal pot on his head and smashed it with a sledgehammer. Zane did his best to show he was fine. With every ounce of strength, he stood up and lied to his coach.

"Yeah, I'm good," he said.

"Why don't we go sit down?"

"Coach, I'm totally fine. It glanced off me. Plus, you need me on the bases. You're out of players."

Rudy looked Zane in the eyes and decided to make up a quick test. "Touch your nose. Now with the other hand. Jump up. Okay, fine, but tell me if your head starts to hurt."

Zane put his helmet back on and patted it. "That's why we wear helmets." He headed to first before Rudy could change his mind. He heard clapping from the stands.

The Bombers' new pitcher was neither as fast nor as big as Moose. On the first pitch, Yuri smacked one to the gap in right-center. Zane burst down the base paths. This was his chance! The crowd was going nuts. Amber scored to tie the game. Zane was approaching third, where Coach Vic held up two hands to stop. Zane smiled and slowed to a stop on the bag.

And heard nothing.

He looked at the bag. He looked at his cleats.

No beeps.

He put his hand to his ear. His mouth opened wide. His earpiece was gone. It must have fallen out when he got hit in the head. Zane looked down toward home plate hoping to spot it. He couldn't see anything. He counted in his head.

Had he been on third long enough?

"Run!" Coach Vic yelled.

Zane stopped calculating and looked back at the action. The Bombers had been trying to catch Yuri in a rundown and made another bad throw. Zane instinctively sprinted for home. The Bombers shortstop fired low to the catcher a step ahead of Zane. From his knees, the catcher turned to apply the tag. Zane leapt clear over the catcher, rolling midair into a somersault. His hands landing on home plate, he completed his roll and popped up by jumping on both feet.

The umpire yelled, *"Safe!"*

Renegades 5, Bombers 4

Zane pumped his fist and let out a yell. It was the coolest thing he had ever done on a baseball field. The victorious Renegades ran out of the dugout and mobbed him. *"Zane! Zane! Zane!"* they cheered, slapping him on the back, helmet, and all over.

Happiness washed over him. Teddy, miraculously healed, was jumping up and down like crazy. "You did it!"

"What about your leg?" Zane shouted above the noise.

Teddy smiled back. "Oh, yeah. Like I said before. I owed you one."

CHAPTER 10

AFTER THE GAME, Rudy gave Zane another speech about being more respectful. He finally ended with a smile, saying, "And hell of a jump, by the way."

Zane thanked him. By the time the conversation was over, most everyone had left. New families were arriving to the fields for the next round of games. Zane had been hoping to catch a ride with one of the teammates on his list. Teddy would have been the easiest to ask, but he was already gone.

He saw Dorian up ahead in the parking lot, and wondered how he'd react if Zane yelled out and asked for a ride. Zane noticed a car pulling up and decided to simply watch. Dorian's mom got out of the car and tried to give him a hug. Dorian shooed her away and got in. His mom said something in another language that caused Dorian to argue back. His mom threw up her hands and got back in the car. This kid was even rude to his own mother.

If that was really her.

Zane was intrigued. What language was that? He regretted not being brave enough to ask for the ride. He wanted to learn more about Dorian, but his head was killing him, and Preston was waiting.

Zane zipped up his bag and headed for home. He was hopeful the walk would help him clear his head and give him time to think. On his way, he imagined explaining to Preston that his high-tech earpiece was now gone. Zane never did see it after the game ended. He knew Preston would also be mad that Zane couldn't figure out a way to go stand on third base for twenty seconds. But Preston was also saying he couldn't arouse any suspicion. So, what was Zane to do?

"There heeeee is."

Zane looked up to see the homeless man, Shorty, blocking the path, smiling. Zane would normally smile back at someone, but the smile coming from Shorty seemed stranger than ever. "Oh, hey," Zane said as he sidestepped the scruffy man, who reeked of alcohol and body odor.

Shorty stepped over to block Zane's path again, then looked around.

"Hey, c'mon," Shorty said. "How about a few bucks?"

"Sorry, I don't—"

Shorty lunged at Zane's legs and knocked him to the ground like an NFL linebacker. Within half a second, Shorty sprung back up and clutched the strap of Zane's baseball backpack. Stunned, Zane realized Shorty wasn't drunk at all but strong, balanced, and aggressive. Shorty jerked hard on the strap. Zane held on.

"What are you doing?" Zane said.

Shorty kept smiling. He leaned back on top of Zane and tried to grab his wrist. Zane's back was pinned to the hot pavement. The guy must have weighed 220 pounds. As Zane struggled to break free, he saw a gun tucked into the man's waistline. Time slowed down. What would this guy do to him once he got the bag?

"Somebody help!" Zane yelled out. He was sure Preston's agents would swoop out of their hiding places and save him.

Nobody came.

Zane squirmed underneath Shorty and finally wriggled his right arm free. He clenched his fist tight and smashed it square into the man's crotch as hard as he could.

The smile finally left Shorty's face. "Ahhggh!" He reached down to grab his groin.

Zane was lightning quick. He slipped out from underneath the wide man and now had the bag to himself. Shorty, however, recovered fast enough to stand up and block Zane's path once again.

Shorty stuck out his hand and growled. "The bag. I could sell that stuff and eat for a week."

Zane remembered a talk his mom gave him last year when she gave him a wallet as a gift. She'd said, "Listen up, Zane-a-lane. No wallet is worth your life. But if anybody ever tried to mug you, never just hand it over. Instead, take out your wallet and throw it as far as you can in one direction, then take off in the other direction. The mugger then has to decide whether to chase you or the wallet. They will choose the wallet, the thing they came for, and by then you will be off to safety and into my arms."

Before Shorty could make another move, Zane flung

his bag as far as he could to his left. Shorty turned to watch it land on a lawn. At that exact moment, Zane sprinted to his right. Shorty reached out to grab him but was too late.

An elderly woman opened the front door, startled. "Hey! I'm calling the police!"

Shorty ran right at her.

"St… St… stop right there," her voice quivered.

To her surprise, Shorty *did* stop—right on her walkway. He scooped up the bag and looked back at the street. Zane was nowhere to be seen.

Zane was running fast. But to where? He had cut between the houses and began to run in a random pattern, the general direction being away from Shorty. Who was that guy? Why did he have a gun? And where were Preston and his agents that were supposed to be watching his back? One thing he knew, he didn't want to go home yet. What if Shorty followed him there? He tucked behind another row of houses near a walking path and took a knee. Thankfully, Zane's phone had been in his pocket. Catching his breath, he fished it out.

Dead. One of these days he would start charging it on a nightly basis. One day. He looked up and realized where he was—one street from Teddy Rempke's.

Dorian, Ricky, Braxton, Erik, Amber, Teddy.

Zane stuck to the path behind the houses and slowly worked his way one block over to where Teddy lived. He eventually got to Teddy's street and remembered which house was his. Zane went around to the front and knocked on the door. Teddy answered, still wearing his uniform from the game.

"Zane?"

"Hey. Is your dad home?"

"Just left for the doctor. What's up? You okay, man?"

Zane stepped in the entryway. He looked back to see if any neighbors were around, then shut the door behind him. "I'm sorry," Zane said.

"For what?"

"For this."

Zane punched Teddy square in the stomach as hard as he could.

CHAPTER II

TEDDY HIT THE entryway floor like a sack of potatoes.

"Wha… wa…." Teddy was trying to say something but had no air.

Zane looked at his friend, deciding he needed to give it a minute before he spoke. Teddy managed to get up on all fours. "What… ehhhhh… the hell?"

Zane raised his voice. "I'm acting on behalf of a Federal Agent with the United States government. We've been on to you the past two weeks."

Teddy could not have looked more confused. He was still on all fours. "So this is… ehhhh… some game?" He gasped again. "You're playing spies, and you slugged me? Ehhh. Screw you. That was way too hard."

Zane needed to push it a bit more. "Nice try. I thought you were my friend. You're nobody's friend. You are a traitor to your entire country. We know about the receiver, the Link, all of it. There are agents at our games watching you. There's one at my house right now. This ends today."

Teddy got up. "Get out. And shut up! Playing some spy thing doesn't give you the right to sucker punch me like that. Ehhhhhh... that hurts. Those guys were right about you. You're a weirdo."

Zane remained quiet, deciding whether to believe him.

"And I thought we were friends," Teddy continued. "You were quitting the team without telling me, then you come by to play some punching game. That's messed up. Go away. And quit the team for all I care."

"I'm sorry," Zane said. "But I had to know."

"Know what?"

"If you were a traitor. I needed to test you. And I need your help."

"Enough!" Teddy threw his hands up. "Aren't you listening? Get out. I don't want to talk to you anymore."

"Everything I was just talking about is true."

"You aren't making any sense," Teddy said. "I don't want to fight you. Leave."

"Okay," Zane said. "I will. Can I please show you something first?"

"What?"

Zane looked down at his feet. Thankfully, he had decided to keep his cleats on. His crocs, glove, bats, along with all the rest of his expensive baseball gear, were in the bag that Shorty stole.

"Your cleats?" Teddy asked. "Did that beanball to the head mess you up? I'll say it again. Leave."

"No, check it out." Zane used his fingernail to pry open a small gap between the shoe and first rubber spike. Zane started to unscrew it. He popped it off and showed Teddy the inside.

"Why is there a computer chip inside your shoe?"

"It's a proximity sensor. And it's not my shoe, it's the government's. Hold on, there's more." Zane worked off the next spike, which revealed another computer chip and the slot housing the micro SD card. "There," Zane said. "Now will you at least listen? You might be more willing to accept my apology."

"Fine. Only because I wanna know what's up with your shoes."

Moments earlier, when Zane realized he was close to Teddy's house, he remembered something. Teddy had said he missed a game last week to go see the Nationals. Zane knew the baseball spy would have to have been there during all the hacks. That, combined with the fact that Teddy simply did not fit the profile—and the way he reacted to the punching test—emboldened Zane to make the calculated risk to trust him all the way. Zane needed help. Teddy was the only guy he remotely trusted, and seemed computer savvy as well. Zane further reasoned that if Teddy *was* the spy, things would have gotten crazy once Zane punched him in the stomach and called him out. It was a pretty backward way of learning how to trust somebody, but it was all Zane could think of while being chased. So, Zane told Teddy the entire story of Preston, his mom, the Cybersecurity Reinforcement Unit and its mission at Falcon Field, and getting jumped. When Zane was done, Teddy stared at the micro SD card.

"Unreal." Teddy shook his head. "I believe you, but I don't forgive you. That was unnecessary. It still kills. For reals."

"At least you believe me. Sorry again. What do I do?"

"Call the police," Teddy said. "Duh."

"I already have the CRU agents. Preston made it sound like the police will mess up the mission if they get involved. This is a delicate dance we're doing here."

"You think Shorty's involved, or was that simply a desperate man stealing a bag?" Teddy asked.

"No idea. Either way, I'm freaked out."

"Fine, let's tell my dad."

"He'll just tell the police," Zane said. "Or he'll get in trouble for knowing about it and not telling the police. We can't tell anybody."

"Fine, whatever. It's got to be Dorian."

"Or Braxton, or Erik, or Ricky, or Amber. Or you."

"Dorian," Teddy repeated. "If anybody's committing treason, it's that guy. Has to be."

"Preston said to keep an open mind on everybody."

Teddy started pacing around, forgetting about his stomach. "What about Yuri? Always on his phone when he's not supposed to be?"

"He's not on the list."

"Oh, yeah," Teddy said.

"Dorian, Braxton, Erik, Ricky, or Amber," Zane said. "I don't know enough about them."

"Ricky and Amber will be easy enough to talk to. Dorian, Braxton, and Erik are the last three guys I would want to get to know. That's bad luck."

Teddy picked up the card.

"There's nothing on it," Zane said. "Remember?"

"You never know." Teddy led Zane to his room and fired up his laptop. He opened his desk drawer and sifted through a tangled mess of cords and chargers.

"Got it! The adapter."

Teddy placed the micro SD card into the adapter, which was the shape and size of a standard SD card. He then slid the adapter into his laptop.

"Okay, now I'm interested," Zane said.

Teddy stared at the screen. "Oh, great."

"What?"

"The blue circle of death. It's fine. I just have to wait for the computer to read this card. This processor sucks. My dad promised me a new one over a year ago."

Zane wondered if he downloaded any files. He also wondered what he would tell Preston.

"There," Teddy said. "It's open. And… we have a file."

"What?"

"We have a file. I guess you were on third long enough after all." The window was open and contained one file—*aht1.mim.*

Teddy continued. "So, you copied this from the receiver that was hidden near or under third base. That means this is a copy of whatever our spy stole from the Link? Am I following this correctly?"

"Yes," Zane said. "So, we can know what the spy found out. What's a 'mim'?"

"If you see that file extension, you better know how to crack an encrypted file."

"So?"

"There. Done."

"For real?" Zane asked.

"For reals. Yeah, it's not that hard once you have the right decrypter program. Take a look. This is really pretty cool stuff."

Zane couldn't believe it. His friend opened the file. It was a black screen with green letters.

"It's an alphabetical list," Zane said. His leg started to bounce with nervous energy.

"Of what?" Teddy asked.

Allyson

Alpha 1

Alpha 2

Artisan

Babcock

Ballerstein

Bama

"Codenames," Zane said. "They look like codenames."

The boys scanned the list.

Frankenstein

Frodo-G

Gallop

Gertie Hurter

Ghost

Teddy stopped scrolling down.

"What?" Zane said. "Keep going."

"If what you said earlier is true, then we're looking at top secret information right now. I shouldn't have done this. These are actual spies for the U.S. government operating in life-or-death undercover situations. We could be arrested for reading this."

"You have a better idea? We have to see what's on this."

Teddy looked back at the screen. He pushed the down arrow, and the screen scrolled down once again, names flashing by.

Otto

Ozzie 1

Ozzie 2

Pats-Mayhew

Paulander

Pavlov

A loud whirring noise came from the other side of the house.

"The garage door!" Teddy said. "My dad! He's back home for some reason."

Robot

Rothschild

~~Rower~~

Roz

Salty

Tisser

"Act natural," Zane said. "Open up another screen if he comes in."

Yellow Bird

Yellowstone Rock

Youngblood

"Teddy?" Mr. Rempke called from the kitchen.

"Back here!" Teddy shouted back. "Zane from the team is over."

Teddy looked at his friend, expecting him to shout out a hello. "Z, say something. Act natural."

Zane couldn't act natural. He couldn't even speak. All he could do is stare at the names at the bottom of the screen.

~~Zane-a-lane 1~~

Zane-a-lane 2

CHAPTER 12

ZANE GRABBED HIS stuff and bolted, barely saying hi to Mr. Rempke on the way out. His heart was racing. He speed walked home, looking out for Shorty while racking his brain.

How?

He thought about all the times he had to move. All the times either his mom or dad had left town on long work trips, usually with no advance notice. On two separate occasions, his dad had been gone for over five months. They told Zane these important "consulting trips" were unpredictable.

Data Analysts?

Yeah, right.

Zane-a-lane 1 and Zane-a-lane 2.

Why didn't they tell him? Why didn't Preston *tell him?*

His anger soon turned into fear. What if his dad's tragic death three years ago in Europe had not been an accident? Did his work get him killed? Zane thought back to when he was only eleven years old, looking at the pictures of the mangled, burned-out car that had left his poor dad unrecognizable. The official investigation ruled it an accident, citing an icy bridge. There had been no connection to any of the work Ryan Clayborn had been doing. Still, Zane imagined the worst.

Zane calmed himself. *Your mom would have told you if she thought someone had killed him. She wouldn't withhold that. And she wouldn't be able to keep that feeling bottled up inside.*

Zane and his mom had been healing and moving forward the past three years, which unfortunately contained two more moves. Once to Fort Meade near Baltimore, and again to Hillandale so she could work out of the CRU offices in Langley. Zane had even started playing baseball again last year in Baltimore. He had a good season. He thought things had settled down. He thought he had things figured out. Then, six weeks ago, they moved again, and now he realized he'd been lied to his entire childhood.

He needed some answers.

When Zane finally arrived home, Preston wasn't even there. Zane charged his phone. A minute later it chirped to life and showed five new messages from Preston. Zane first tried reaching his mom, but the call went straight to voicemail. His emotions ranged from pride to betrayal. He thought about calling Preston but decided he needed to sort out his story before the two spoke. Zane listened to his messages. Each were short, angry demands for Zane to call him as soon as possible. Five minutes later, Preston pulled into the driveway. He was wearing a navy bowtie that perfectly matched his blazer. Zane opened the door to let him in.

"Where were you?" Preston said, not bothering to conceal his anger. "I had to go drive around the block. And you didn't even have your phone!"

"It died. But where were you before that? I thought you and your agents were watching me."

"They watched the game, then left. Too early, apparently. What happened? Where have you been?"

"Is my mom a spy?" Zane asked. "Was my dad? Was he murdered?"

"What?" Preston asked. "Why would you think that?"

"She's a spy, and so was he. Right? I know it."

"What?"

"I downloaded a file. Codenames. I read it."

Preston's expression changed immediately. "Listen. You are playing with fire here. This is not a game. You were supposed to hand over whatever you got. Give me the micro SD card right now, and tell me exactly what happened."

"I'm not talking until you tell me what's going on," Zane said.

"Give me the file," Preston repeated.

Zane folded his arms.

"It's better if you don't know," Preston said.

"I already know. If you want me to talk, you need to talk first."

Preston looked down at the table and rubbed his temples. "There's more to the CRU than you realize. Your mom wants you to think she has a desk job because it's safer that way. Your dad kept up the same act when he was alive. Why do you think they misled you all these years?"

Zane didn't know what to say.

Preston continued. "Ryan Clayborn was one of the best undercover agents the CRU ever had. I'm so sorry you lost him. We all lost him. But put that scary thought about his death to rest. It was an accident. We investigated the crash thoroughly. So did your mom. And Mallory Clayborn is one of the best. So yes, she's undercover. They both began this life before you were born. And yes, it's as dangerous as it sounds."

Zane had a thousand more questions. "So, what's she do?" was the first that came to his lips.

"Whatever the United States needs. She risks her life to build relationships. She earns trust so she can gather crucial intel overseas, find cyberterrorists, arms dealers, you name it. She helps our leaders make life-or-death decisions. And now you know how serious the situation is at Falcon Field. Do you realize what this new development means?"

Zane was still trying to wrap his brain around everything. "Yeah."

"Well, in case you don't, her code name is compromised. That means her current mission is probably over. And if our baseball spy steals the last file and the key to match them up, then your mom's true identity would be revealed to some pretty bad people—people who will then be coming for you and your mom. I didn't want to scare you like this. You're no good to us if you are a nervous wreck."

Zane was trying to take it all in.

Preston continued. "At the very least, you'll both have to change your names, leave town, leave your friends."

"I don't have any friends." Zane felt silly saying it, since the bigger issue was an angry terrorist getting a list with his family's name on it.

"Zane, the Cybersecurity Reinforcement Unit is very effective. We're here to handle this threat at Falcon Field. I need the file now."

"Well, I need to talk to my mom now."

"I wish I could do that for you," Preston said, softening a bit. "I know you want to talk to her about everything, but it's simply not possible. We still need her help on this, and security is extreme. I promise we can talk to her as soon as this blows over. We have to find this spy and gather information. Do you know how many lives are at stake? I need that file so I can take a look at what they have. The sooner we figure all this out, the sooner your mom comes home."

Zane sighed. "Hold on." He went over to the closet and brought back his left baseball cleat. He placed it on the table and opened up the spike, just like he had at Teddy's. He took out the micro SD card and gave it to Preston.

"How did you read this file?" Preston asked. "Where'd you go after the game?"

"There was a man," Zane said. "He, he…."

Zane started to tell him what happened but choked on his words. The tears came from nowhere. He finally had a second to think back, and the fear and anxiety caught up to him. It felt like a boulder was crushing his chest.

Preston had no idea what to say. He started to place his hand on Zane's shoulder but decided to pull it back.

"Hey, now. You're okay. Your mom's going to be okay. We can get through this. Talk to me."

Zane recovered and wiped his nose. "Sorry. I was attacked on the way home."

"By who? What happened?"

"We call him 'Shorty.' I guess he's this homeless guy who hangs around near the field. I was walking home, and he approached me. Nobody else was around, so he must have thought it would be his chance to steal something from me. He went for my bag. He said he could sell the stuff inside and eat for a week. I tried to go around him, and out of nowhere, he jumped on top of me. He was holding me down, and then I saw he had a gun tucked inside his waistband."

"He had a gun?"

"He didn't pull it out, but I flipped. It all happened so fast, but I was able to hit him hard in the nuts and slip out. I ended up throwing the bag to the side. He went for it, and I escaped. I ran like hell, and then hid in an alley."

"You hit him in the nuts?"

"Yeah. Hard."

Preston grinned. "Nice."

"So, is this connected?" Zane asked, calming down.

"I really don't think so. People carry guns, even crazies. What happened next?"

"I got home, and you weren't here, so I loaded the file," Zane lied. "I used my dad's old computer to read it. He taught me how to decrypt stuff."

"Why didn't you wait for me, or call me? I was driving around looking for you."

"I don't know. I guess I wanted to make sure I saw it. I was worried you'd keep the info from me. Which you would have."

Zane was challenging Preston's authority, but Preston let it slide.

Zane continued. "But either way, here I am with my mom on a list and a crazy guy looking for me."

"What did he look like?"

"Really short and stocky. Half-black, half-white, I think. Dark, curly hair, hasn't shaved in a while."

"I promise I'll talk to every one of our agents and get to the bottom of this." Preston took out his laptop and popped in the micro SD card. His machine didn't need an adapter. He looked at the list. "Codenames. You're right. This is bad, but our culprit doesn't have the identities or the key. We still have time to identify the spy and let him lead us to whoever he's working for. The overall mission can be a success. You have to get back out there. ID the spy. See if the receiver has been active."

"Without getting caught," Zane said.

"You've come this far."

"What about Shorty?"

"I'll add another plain clothes agent," Preston said. "If Shorty tries something, they'd be on him in a heartbeat."

"Where were they today?"

"They gave you too much room. I'll talk to them. We need to go back. You have another game tomorrow. Watch third base like a hawk. Watch your teammates. Get them talking. Ask them about their families. See which story sounds like a lie. What's the latest on that front?"

"I found out who's new on the team this year," Zane said.

Preston perked up. "That's good. Really good. You should have told me sooner." Preston took out a pad, clicked a pen, and handed both over. Zane jotted down the names he had committed to memory. *Dorian Delini, Ricky Martinez, Braxton Greiner, Erik Olsson, Amber Hyatt, T—*

As soon as he started to write down Teddy's name, he stopped, mad at himself for his mistake. All he had written was a "*T*." He scratched it out.

"Is that it?" Preston asked.

Zane thought for a moment. "Yeah." He changed the subject. "I still don't know if this is going to work."

"I think you need a reminder," Preston said. "Imagine what it's like for an international agent, working undercover with murderous, unpredictable thugs who are after nuclear weapons. Now imagine what those murderous thugs would do if they found out their 'friend' is actually an American undercover agent."

"Kill them?"

Preston nodded. "Without hesitation. And don't think of these agents as just faceless, nameless people we're trying to save, Zane. One of them is your mom."

CHAPTER 13

TUESDAY MORNING WAS tough. What made it hard, oddly enough, was not having Preston around to talk to. Preston left early in the morning and said he'd be in touch. Zane spent the morning looking out the window, wondering if there were agents watching him.

Around 2:30, Preston came home and chatted again about the mission, mostly reviewing what they had been over. He told Zane he couldn't offer him a ride to the game because he didn't want to be seen with Zane near the field. The other agents, Zane was told, were already in position. Zane went to his room, put on his uniform, laced up some running shoes, and held his computerized cleats in his hands. He left his bedroom, shut the door, and closed it on the way out. He saw Preston wasn't looking, so Zane turned around and faced his bedroom door. He opened it a crack and inserted a toothpick between the doorframe and the side of the door near the hinges. Then he shut the door and broke off the part of the toothpick that was sticking out. He could barely see the remainder of the toothpick still wedged in the door. Satisfied, he headed for the front door and said goodbye to Preston.

Once outside, Zane couldn't see anybody watching him, so he went ahead with his own plan. After he reached the next street, he casually cut west between two houses and emerged on another block. He spun around in all directions, careful to see if anyone followed. He continued west, cutting one more block through two more houses, then headed north to the intersection where Teddy was waiting.

"Present for you." Teddy handed Zane his extra bat bag, which contained a glove, batting gloves, and bat.

"Thanks," Zane said.

"Of course. Least I could do for you after you socked me in the stomach."

Zane smiled. "But seriously, did you see anybody watching me?"

"No. No agents here."

"It's not the agents I'm worried about," Zane said. The boys began walking to the field.

"Shorty's long gone," Teddy said. "He figures you called the cops on him, so he has to find a new place to hang out. Right now, he's someplace else, worried about getting arrested."

"Yeah, but what if he's not?"

"It only takes a couple of seconds to dial nine-one-one," Teddy said.

"Why am I even doing this? I just want this whole thing to be over."

"You still can't talk to your mom?"

"As soon as I can, I am going to let her have it though." Zane's volume was gradually rising. "She kept me in the dark this whole time, and look where it led. Some guy wants to jump me, and if I can't pull this off, we'll be on a terrorist's hit list."

"You might want to chill. Never know who's listening. And I'm not supposed to be in the loop here, remember? Preston would kill you."

Zane looked over at him.

"Sorry, bad choice of words," Teddy said.

"Fine."

The boys arrived at the edge of the Falcon Field parking lot.

"But one more thing," Teddy said. "Here's what I don't get. If you are Preston, you know where the receiver is. It's under third base somewhere. You know what it could do. The spy already has one file. At what point do you stop worrying about tipping off the spy and just go end the threat?"

"I know," Zane said. "It's a pretty big risk for him to take. It's my family on the line. But I guess the bigger risk is letting the spy get away without knowing their plan."

"I don't like it," Teddy said.

"I just have to finish the job fast," Zane said. "What choice do I have?"

"You've got me helping. I'll keep my eyes on those five at all times."

"Dorian, Ricky, Braxton, Erik, and Amber," Zane said. "Learn as much as you can."

"Dorian, Ricky, Braxton, Erik, and Amber," Teddy repeated to himself.

They crossed the parking lot and headed past the outfield wall of Diamond One. Now it was Teddy that looked nervous.

"Try to act cool," Zane said. "Remember, the most important thing is that nobody can know what we're up to."

"Acting cool," Teddy said with a nod.

"Teddy!" Rudy shouted.

Teddy jumped out of his skin. "Oh, hey Coach."

"How's your dad doing?" Rudy asked.

"Eh. Thanks for asking though."

"I just found out," Rudy said. "You should have told me sooner. Will you let me know if you need anything?"

"I will. It's kinda hard to talk about."

"It doesn't have to be," Rudy said. "I'm serious. We're your family out here. Anytime you want to talk."

"Thanks," Teddy said. "There actually is one thing."

"What is it?"

"Ricky said his parents were going to give me something for my dad. This is sort of embarrassing, but I don't know who his parents are. Can you point them out?"

"Right over there." Rudy pointed to a couple settling into their seats. "Amaya and Juan. That doesn't surprise me they want to help. They're great. I actually knew them five years ago before they moved away the first time."

"Perfect. Thanks again."

Rudy said hello to Zane and then headed onto the field. Zane looked at Teddy with concern.

"Lung cancer," Teddy explained.

"Oh, man," Zane said. "I'm really sorry. You should've told me."

"I was going to, but we already had a lot going on."

"How bad is it?"

"Could be a lot better," Teddy said. "They hope the treatment will get it all, but the uncertainty sucks. It really, really sucks."

Zane looked at Teddy, not sure what to say.

Teddy spoke quietly. "You lost your dad, didn't you? That's why 'Zane-A-Lane 1' was crossed out?"

"I know what you're thinking. But he wasn't killed by some bad guy. It was a random car accident while he was away. Three years ago. Worst luck in the world."

"I'm really sorry, man. How are you coping?"

"I'll never get over it, but we're finally learning to live with it," Zane said. He noticed how scared Teddy suddenly looked. "Look, you aren't going to need tips from me on how to cope with loss. Don't go there. Just because I lost my dad doesn't mean you're losing yours."

Teddy broke eye contact and blushed. "You don't know that."

It was true, and Zane wasn't sure what to say.

Teddy pounded his fist in his glove and looked out at the field. "Let's worry about today."

"Ricky, Dorian, Braxton, Erik, and Amber," Zane said.

Zane looked over his shoulder at some parents arriving and turned back to Teddy. "If you don't mind me asking, where's your mom?"

"I thought you trusted me," Teddy said.

"Sorry," Zane said. "I didn't mean to—"

"It's fine." Teddy interrupted. "That's one of the reasons I'm so scared about my dad. He's all I got. I don't even know what I'd do or where I'd go. Then I feel guilty for thinking about myself."

"Those are normal feelings, and I'm telling you, you guys are gonna be all right."

Teddy didn't look convinced but nodded anyway.

"And my mom's all I got," Zane said. "So, let's do this. Ricky, Dorian, Braxton, Erik, and Amber. And I need to go stand on third for twenty seconds."

"Actually, cross Ricky off the list," Teddy said.

"Huh?"

"I know we got sidetracked with the deep stuff there—and thanks for that—but I totally made that up about Ricky's parents so we could get some intel."

"Impressive," Zane said, nodding.

"Did you catch what Rudy said? Amaya and Juan know Rudy from five years ago. The family lived here and came back. With Ricky."

"And if Rudy wasn't enough of an alibi, the family size is the clincher," Zane said. "A kid with two parents at the games is less likely, because each of the parents would have to be fake."

"Plus, how would you explain that?" Teddy motioned to the bleachers. A six-year-old girl, presumably Ricky's little sister, was crying for an iPad.

"Okay, this is good," Zane said. "Ricky's out. We're getting somewhere. So, out of Dorian, Braxton, Erik, and Amber, we figure out which of them has one or zero parents show up."

"Exactly."

"At least it's a plan," Zane said.

Teddy straightened up. "Dorian, Braxton, Erik, and Amber. And then there were four."

The boys walked toward the field. Time to act. Preston had supplied Zane with a new earpiece. Zane never found the old one, which made him nervous, but he definitely had more confidence than the first time he'd done this. The micro SD card was back in his cleats. Zane was planning on going right for the base as soon as he could work it into the normal flow of the game, and then he'd watch Dorian, Braxton, Erik, and Amber for a reaction.

As they got to the field, however, Zane saw he was not in luck. His teammates were settling into the first base dugout. He was hoping for the third base dugout, which meant his team would have been warming up right near third base. Zane and Teddy walked in. Zane heard a beep, and then listened hard for the next one, even though he already knew where his target was.

Zane wasn't able to keep his focus for long. Jamal, the Atwater twin with a big smile and braces, slapped Zane on the back. "What's the matter, slugger?"

"What do you mean?"

"Thought you looked upset. Even more high-strung than usual."

"Nope, just want to play well today," Zane said.

"Yeah, we actually need this one really bad," Jamal said.

Teddy gave Zane a nudge with his elbow and motioned toward the end of the dugout. Dorian was lacing up his cleats. As he leaned over, a thin gold chain dangled below his chin. Zane knew he'd have to talk to Dorian eventually, so he might as well try now.

Zane walked over and cleared his throat. "Hey, man."

"Hey," Dorian answered, eyes focused down on his double knot.

"So, what language were you speaking the other day?" Zane asked.

Dorian looked up like he had been caught stealing cookies. "What are you talking about?"

"Oh, nothing. I heard you and your mom, that's all."

"Italian." He got up to leave, but Zane persisted.

"Cool," Zane said, trying to buy himself a second to think. "I know this is random. My mom thinks she recognized your mom from her office. It's a big office. She was curious if they worked together. Where does your mom work?"

"What's this? Twenty questions?"

Zane couldn't tell if Dorian was joking or actually annoyed. "Just chatting, man."

"Insurance," Dorian said. "Some insurance office. I dunno where."

Zane gave up. "That's not it, never mind."

"Guys, get out there!" Rudy yelled.

Each team had begun warming up at the same time. The Panthers were on the third base line, extending to left field. The Renegades were on the first base line, extending into right.

"Hey, Teddy," Amber called out.

"Hey," Teddy said back. "Uh… how's it going?"

"Good. Let's toss."

"My arm is kinda sore. I better not."

"Seriously?"

Teddy shrugged.

"Ah-ight," she said. "Hope it feels better."

"I need a partner," Dorian said, holding up a ball.

Erik had been about to start tossing with Dorian.

Amber looked at Erik and hesitantly agreed. "Sure," she said.

"Great, let's see what you got," Dorian said in a chipper voice. "Sorry, Erik!"

"Whatever," Erik said.

Zane saw an opportunity. He tossed a ball lightly at Erik. "You wanna toss?"

Erik caught it. "Not really."

"You sure?" Zane asked. There was nobody else left but Zane and Teddy, and Teddy was sitting on the bench like a lump. Zane let the uncomfortable silence linger. It worked.

"Fine," Erik said. He got up and flipped the ball back to Zane. The two boys went out to the field and began playing catch. Erik threw it as hard as he could.

"What's the problem?" Zane asked.

"Nothing." Erik threw it back, but Zane purposely missed it. The ball started rolling toward the middle of the infield. Erik groaned. Zane gave chase, waiting to hear the "beep" from third base.

Nothing. He took a few giant steps toward third and slid his thumb on his belt, making sure the volume was all the way up.

Silence.

"You went right past it!" Erik yelled. "You wear glasses or something?"

"Sorry!" Zane ran back toward the mound to get the ball. He threw one right on the money to Erik. It made a perfect "pop" in his glove. Zane jogged back to his spot and picked up where they left off.

"Nice throw," Erik said before throwing it back at a regular speed.

"Thanks." Zane casually touched his belt again to make sure the volume was up. He knew the earpiece was working because he heard the static hissing loudly in his ear. Just no "beep."

Sensing he couldn't get anywhere with Erik, Zane turned his sights to Braxton Greiner, who was next to him, throwing down toward Mateo Perez.

"You think we got these guys?" Zane asked Braxton.

"Yeah, they don't look very good."

"Do we?" Zane asked.

"We look better than that. As long as you keep doing your ninja moves on the base paths."

This was the first time Braxton had been nice to Zane all season. Maybe being separated from Erik and Dorian was key. Zane decided to go for it.

"Hey, you want to hang tomorrow night? Play video games or something?"

Braxton looked over to see how closely Erik was watching. "Maybe."

"Oh wait," Zane said. "My mom's gone. I am not supposed to have anybody over. Maybe your house?"

"I don't know, I'll see. It might work."

"Cool."

Braxton threw the ball back to Mateo and yelled out, "I'm good!" He jogged to the dugout without saying anything else to Zane.

"PANTHERS' FIELD!" Rudy yelled. The Renegades all filed back to the dugout, except for Teddy, who had never left his seat on the end of the bench. Zane went and sat by him. The rest of the Renegades were fiddling with their helmets, bats, and sunflower seeds. Rudy yelled

out the lineup. Zane was batting fifth today and playing centerfield. So much for an easy path to third base.

Zane kept sitting by Teddy, waiting for the right moment to talk. Finally, he whispered the update. "Something's up with the receiver. I don't hear the beeps."

"Were you close enough?" Teddy asked. "Get closer and see what happens."

"I'm trying," Zane said. "Oh, and get this. Dorian says he speaks Italian, then got all defensive, in case you didn't hear. Plus, I finally got somewhere with Braxton. I asked him to hang out. We might go to his house. With any luck we can cross him off."

"What if he only has one parent there?" Teddy said. "What if he's still lying?"

"I guess we'll see soon enough. What was that with Amber back there?"

"I can't do this," he said. "I can barely breathe. You'll have to deal with her. I'm too nervous."

"Don't you remember what's at stake?" Zane asked. "You realize she could be trying to get Americans killed."

"All the more reason not to talk to her," Teddy said.

"We need you." Zane pressed on while Teddy stared ahead into space. "You think I wanted to talk to Dorian and Braxton like that? If you can somehow ask her on a date, you could find out all about her."

"A date?!" Teddy shrieked.

Zane looked around to see if anybody heard. "Keep it down."

"You're dreaming," Teddy said. "Kind of a big difference between you asking Braxton to hang out and me asking Amber on a date."

"This is your perfect chance to act. It's all to help the mission, so it's totally the same as me and Braxton. Plus, I know talking to girls isn't easy, so thinking about the mission takes all the pressure off."

"Or puts way more on," Teddy said.

Ricky and Sammy came back in and sat down next to Zane, ending his chance to talk to Teddy about the plan.

"You see those warmup pitches?" Sammy said, looking at the Panthers pitcher.

"My grandma could hit this dude," Mateo said.

"You're grandma's pretty scary looking though," Sammy said.

Zane looked back at Teddy with hope in his eyes.

Teddy relaxed his shoulders and nodded. "You owe me," he whispered to Zane.

Zane smiled and nodded back. He just hoped Teddy had the guts to go through with it.

Rudy laughed at something Ches said, then cleared his throat. "Take your positions!" Rudy let everyone know the Renegades would start their final warmups, with first pitch to follow. The players were all heading out to their spots in the field, but Teddy didn't move.

"Are your legs still broken?" Zane said.

"Not in the lineup."

All twelve guys showed up for the game that day. Teddy, Cedric Atwater, and Yuri Sokolov would have to wait for Rudy to sub them in.

"Gotcha," Zane said. "I'm sure you'll find the right moment for you-know-what."

Teddy smiled as confidently as he could, not really believing he was about to ask *Amber Hyatt* on a date.

Zane, meanwhile, headed out of the dugout, just in time to hear Dorian and Amber talking in front of him.

"...so what do you think?" Dorian asked. "Tomorrow night? Is it a date?"

"I'll let you take me out," Amber said, "but only *if* we win this game."

"You're on," Dorian said.

CHAPTER 14

AS ZANE JOGGED out to centerfield, his first thought was not about how his fellow agent may have just lost his golden chance to learn more about Amber. No, it was about his sensitive friend who was about to ask a girl on a date for the first time ever—and probably shouldn't.

It was Ricky's day to pitch. He took the mound, popped a bubble, and started his warmups. Zane jogged past and shook his head. When he got to centerfield, he knew for sure something was wrong.

Beep!

The first beep. Zane didn't hear it until he got into the outfield. His earpiece should have been beeping faster when he was passing the mound, close to third base. He wandered to his left a bit toward Amber in left field.

BEEP!Beep!

The beeps increased each time he went further into left.

Zane knew he had to make another download. He also knew he had to figure out whether it was Dorian,

Braxton, Erik, or Amber behind all this. If he could do that, maybe he could convince Preston to come in, get the receiver, and arrest the baseball spy. His mom might even be home in time for dinner.

Zane looked back into the dugout and saw Teddy looking at him. Zane mouthed, "It moved."

"Hey, did you forget you're in center?" Amber asked.

"Just stretching my legs." Zane turned and jogged in a wide circle around his spot in center, and then settled into his position.

"PLAY BALL!" the umpire yelled.

Ricky's first pitch was right down the middle and fast. The Panthers' leadoff batter swung so hard he lost his grip, sending the bat flying toward Dorian, who was playing third. Dorian, however, didn't dive out of the way. Instead, he reached out and grabbed the bat. The Renegades' fans cheered. Dorian took a step toward home and tossed the bat back to the Panthers' batter.

"Wow!" yelled Amber from left. "That was so cool."

"A little dumb also, maybe," Zane said to Amber.

"You know he's not that bad. You just don't understand him."

"I didn't say Dorian was bad. But are you trying to convince me or yourself?"

Crack!

The ball was headed toward center. Zane had it lined up and made the easy catch.

"One away!" Zane yelled as he trotted back toward his place in the outfield.

"Okay, I get it," Amber said, picking up the conversation. "You heard him ask me out. What do you care?"

Dink!

A grounder to short. Braxton scooped it up and fired to Erik for out number two.

"Sorry," Zane said. "I didn't mean to eavesdrop. I was right there. It seems weird after the way he treated you."

"He didn't 'treat' me like anything. We just never really talked that much. You and Teddy don't talk to me, either. Nobody does. "

The conversation paused as Ricky began to pitch to the next batter. He was a kid nicknamed "Ribs" because he was so skinny. He was also fast. Ribs hit a slow grounder to third. Dorian never had a chance. Ribs was safe by a mile. Zane and Amber had each rushed up a few steps but were now returning to their spots.

"You're right," Zane said. "I could have been friendlier. But I wasn't trying to be mean, honest. I was being shy. I'm having some problems of my own."

"Sounds just like Dorian," she said. "Either way, if we lose this game you won't have to see anybody the rest of the summer."

"What do you mean?"

The next man up, Scott Beadle, crushed a liner right at Amber. She charged hard at the ball and dove for it. The ball skipped past her and began hopping toward the wall, building steam like a runaway train. Ribs was already rounding second. As the crowd cheered, Zane sprinted to the wall behind Amber.

BEEP! BEEP! BEEP! BEEP!

Zane grabbed the ball, spun and fired to the cutoff man, Braxton, at short. Ribs scored. Scotty had himself an RBI double.

BEEEEEEP!

It was so loud it sounded like a tone. Zane froze. He was in range. He started to count to twenty in his head. Amber got to her feet and looked up at Zane.

"Good effort," Zane said, trying to act natural. "Almost made SportsCenter with that one."

"Almost." Amber smiled. She started to walk back to her spot.

Zane immediately dropped to a knee and acted like he was tying his shoe. Amber looked at him funny again. "Well, we won't be playing anymore past today if we can't make a few plays," she said.

SWOOOOSH! Zane heard the signal. Download complete. He smiled, finished pretend-tying his shoes, and started back to his spot.

"Wait, what?" he asked.

"The playoffs," Amber said. "That's what I was talking about before. We don't make the playoffs unless we win today. You didn't know that?"

"Oh my gosh, you're right. I didn't look all that closely at the end of the schedule once I decided to...."

"Decided to quit?"

The crowd cheered. The next batter, Jake Holloway, hit a liner down the line in right. Amber and Zane didn't even have to move. They watched Mateo give chase in right while Scott scored to make it 2-0 Panthers.

"The rest of the games after this are all postseason," she said.

"Yeah, I get it," Zane said, sounding a lot meaner that he intended.

"If we make it. But you were quitting, anyway."

"Well, I decided to play," he said. "And if I'm playing, I'm playing to win."

"Fair enough. Learn to read, though, it might come in handy."

While Zane was processing this new info, he watched Ricky strike out the next batter.

The Renegades jogged to the dugout, down 2-0 to one of the worst teams in the league.

"Settle down Renegades," Rudy said. "Our turn, now. Here we go."

When Zane came into the dugout, Teddy was sitting next to Jamal and Cedric Atwater.

"You guys realize that we miss the playoffs if we don't win this one?" Zane said.

"Uh, yeah," Jamal said. "I guess Cedric isn't the only one not listening when coach is talking."

Cedric picked up a bottle and took off the cap. "This your Gatorade?" he asked his brother. He spit in his chewed up sunflower seeds.

"Actually, it's Rudy's," Jamal said. "Mine's in my bag."

The team burst out laughing. Rudy had headed out to coach third base, completely unaware.

Zane brought them back to reality. "Guys! If there's anything we wanted to accomplish this year, we better do it now."

Teddy nodded.

"Relax, we're not losing to the Panthers," Sammy said.

Zane had to figure out a way to talk to Teddy. "You know that app I was telling you about? I was able to download it."

"Really," Teddy said. "Cool. I can't wait to see it."

Zane threw his coach's Gatorade bottle in the trash can at the end of the dugout.

Erik looked annoyed. "What are you doing?"

"Saving Cedric," Zane said.

A few more innings went by before Zane had a second alone with Teddy. Teddy had left the dugout to track down a foul ball. Zane walked out to meet him upon his return.

"Bad news," Zane said. "Dorian asked Amber on a date for tomorrow night. I've been trying to tell you."

Teddy was taken aback. "What? When?"

"Right as the game started. She told him, 'only if we win.' It's like a bet or something. I'm sorry, man, but I thought you should know."

"So, if we lose, she doesn't go out with him," Teddy said hopefully.

"We have to win," Zane said. "This is for the playoffs. Is it Dorian, Braxton, Erik, or Amber? We need more time!"

"Okay, okay." Teddy said. "Chill out. We're gonna win easily. I'll help you find the spy, and then ask her out on my own terms. You're really messing with my head, you realize that?"

"I owe you," Zane said. "Thanks."

But it wasn't easy at all. The Renegades were playing one of their worst games of the season. Since pitch count rules required Dorian to wait four days until he could pitch again, the team was unable to use their top pitcher. Ricky was struggling. He was walking batters, and the defense was making errors, allowing all those runners to score. Sammy came in as the next pitcher but did not fare any better. As they headed to the bottom of the seventh and final inning, the Panthers were winning 11-10.

The Renegades were up to bat, and they had to score. Braxton started the inning by getting a base hit to center-field. The ball rolled through Ribs's legs.

"Take two!" Rudy yelled, waving his arm frantically.

Braxton rounded first and sprinted for second. But Ribs was too fast. He found the ball right away and threw a perfect ball to second. Braxton slid in hard and screamed.

He somehow managed to avoid the tag but rolled his ankle in the process.

"Safe!" yelled the ump. "Coach!"

Rudy and Coach Ches ran out together to take a look at Braxton, who was fighting back tears. He was taking deep breaths.

"There go my plans with Braxton," Zane said to Teddy.

"Doesn't matter," Teddy said. "Look. This is even better."

A pair of adults, along with a young boy and girl, appeared behind the dugout.

Rudy and Coach Ches were helping Braxton limp off the field.

"Braxton, sweetie," the woman said.

"Mom, I'm okay!" he said.

Jamal and Cedric looked at each other. "That probably hurt worse than the ankle," Cedric said.

Braxton managed to get to the grassy area behind the dugout and have a seat. His parents were talking to him and deciding what to do. Zane and Teddy looked at each other and understood. Braxton had a whole family. He was off the list.

Dorian, Erik, or Amber.

"Yuri," Rudy said. "Pinch run for Braxton."

The Panthers' pitcher, Chris, melted under the pressure. He walked Ricky, then Erik. The bases were loaded with nobody out. Dorian walked up to the plate and gave Amber a wink.

"Gimme a break," Teddy said.

Dorian swung at the first pitch he saw, lining it right at the pitcher, who caught it. The Panthers all cheered. The Renegades all groaned. Dorian looked back at Amber in the dugout and smiled. "Close."

Sammy came up next but only managed a grounder to third. The third baseman threw home to get Yuri out. The runners advanced, but the Renegades were still down a run and down to their final out.

The Renegades' next batter stepped to the plate. This was it. The Renegades were down 11-10, with two outs in the final inning. Zane's season, his mission, and his family were all on the line. Everyone looked at the kid stepping up to the plate, the kid that subbed in an inning earlier.

The voice crackled over the speakers. *"Now batting for the Renegades... number two, Teddy Rempke."*

CHAPTER 15

"COME ON, TEDDY!" Amber yelled.

Teddy walked to the batter's box and looked back at Amber. Then he looked over at Dorian.

"Let's do it here, Two, we need this!" Dorian said.

Teddy had no expression at all as he looked at his teammate. He stepped into the box and placed his bat gently on his back shoulder. Chris, who was not throwing hard all game, was getting tired. He threw a meatball right down the middle. Teddy stood there and watched it go by.

The umpire shouted, *"Strike!"* even though everybody already knew.

"Let's go, Teddy!" Zane said. Zane started to wonder if his friend would really lose on purpose. Maybe since they had narrowed it down to three suspects, Teddy figured they had done enough. If so, he was making a deadly mistake—deadly for Zane's family. Zane was hoping Teddy would look over to the dugout and see the concern on his face.

Chris made his next pitch. This one was knee high, just asking to get swatted.

Teddy didn't flinch.

"Strike two!" yelled the ump.

"Be a hitter now, Rempke!" Rudy yelled.

Jamal followed. "Hit that!"

The place started to go quiet as the tension built. The Renegades were down to their final strike. Chris waited for the sign, narrowed his eyes, and put the ball near his belt. Then they all heard it.

"Girllll, you on my pro-pro-fiiiiiile."

Everybody laughed.

The latest Chandler DeNario song had begun blaring from the Renegades' dugout. There was a flurry of activity as several of the players scrambled to find out where exactly it was coming from. Phones were definitely not allowed in the dugout. Teddy stepped out of the box and called for time.

"Sorry, I thought it was off!" he yelled to his teammates. "It's mine. Blue Mizuno bag."

Zane was trying to make eye contact with Teddy, but Teddy wasn't looking his direction. He had already started walking back to the box.

"Hey, Teddy, even CDN wants you to swing!" Ricky yelled from second base.

Teddy's eyes lit up at the comment. He looked at Zane with a sudden burst of intensity. He waited half a second, then stepped into the box. He relaxed his breathing and focused on Chris.

Zane and the rest of the Renegades were on their feet. The crowd noise steadily built again. Chris delivered the

0-2 pitch. It was way outside, but Teddy went for it, waving the bat out and barely fouling it back.

"At least he swung that time," Cedric said to Zane.

Mateo leaned in from the other side. "It's like he finally woke up."

The next pitch was right down the middle. Once again, Teddy was swinging. Except this time, his rhythm was perfect.

The ball went right back where it came from. It whistled over the mound, past Chris, and into centerfield for a base hit. Yuri ran home easily to tie it. Ricky was right behind him.

Rudy was whipping his arm around like a windmill. "Score! Score!" he yelled as the fans cheered like crazy. Ricky rounded third. In shallow centerfield, Ribs got to the ball in a flash, then picked it up and threw home in one fluid motion. Ricky saw the catcher shift to the first base side to catch the throw from center. In that split second, Ricky decided to slide wide to the outside of the plate. The catcher caught the ball and swept his arm back toward Ricky but got nothing but air. As Ricky's feet and body slid a foot right of the plate, he reached out his left arm, careful to avoid the catcher's mitt, and dragged his hand across the dish for the winning run.

"*Safe!*"

Renegades 12, Panthers 11
Playoff game on Thursday

The Renegades all raced toward the plate to greet Ricky, then immediately toward first, where Teddy was jumping up and down. Zane joined in, feeling like an elephant had been removed from his chest.

"Teddy! Teddy! Teddy!" his teammates chanted.

"It was all for CDN!" he said. His teammates thought that was hilarious.

Moments later, the team was exiting the dugout. Zane and Teddy's thoughts returned to Dorian, Erik, and Amber.

Teddy elbowed Zane and pointed. "Check it out."

Up ahead, Erik and Dorian were walking to the parking lot with Erik's dad. There were no other parents around. Amber was tagging along.

"That doesn't really show us anything," Zane said.

"Maybe, but that file hidden in your cleats sure will," Teddy replied.

They watched from afar as Amber said goodbye to Dorian. They could see Dorian say something that looked and sounded like, "Tomorrow night," which made Amber grin and scrunch her shoulders. Zane looked at Teddy, who pretended not to care.

"Hey," Zane said, "I know you got that hit for me. Thanks, man."

"Actually, I did it because I figured out who's gonna fix all this."

"Who's that?"

"Chandler DeNario," Teddy said.

Zane chuckled. "Right, of course."

Teddy grinned and raised his eyebrows twice.

"Teddy, what the hell are you talking about?"

CHAPTER 16

HE COULD HAVE walked home with Teddy, but the more time he spent with his friend, the greater chance Preston might suspect Teddy knew about the mission. So, Zane told Teddy he would see him at tomorrow's practice, then decided to walk separately.

When Zane got home, he was very eager to see if Preston had gone into his room and snooped around. Zane went to his room and saw the tiny piece of toothpick still poking out of the door frame at the correct spot. His toothpick alarm told him that Preston had not opened the door to his room. Had that been the case, then the toothpick would have fallen out onto the ground. Zane appreciated Preston honoring his privacy. Next, Zane did as instructed. He walked directly to his couch, opened up his laptop, took out his phone, and dialed Preston, who was at work waiting.

Preston answered on the first ring. *"Are you okay?"*

"Yeah, I'm fine. I made another download."

"We need to hang up and switch to computers," Preston said. *"Click 'yes' when the prompt comes up."*

Zane's computer screen signaled an incoming call. It also said, *USER WISHES TO TAKE CONTROL OF SCREEN. ALLOW?*

Zane clicked *ACCEPT* and *YES.*

Preston's face popped up on the screen, and he resumed the conversation. *"Real quick. I've been feeling really bad about putting you in this situation. I wish I knew a better way. I want you to know I had three men on you today in case anything happened. They didn't see anybody suspicious. Oh, and I'll hopefully be back at your place by nine tonight."*

"Thanks. I'm fine," Zane said. "I am more worried about what's on this card. If the baseball spy has another file, that means my mom is one step closer to being completely exposed. And we're still letting the spy continue to hack. So, if my card shows they have made progress, then can we finally end all this?"

"Let's not get ahead of ourselves. First things first. Tell me what happened."

Zane didn't appreciate that Preston dodged his question but decided to let it go for the time being. "They moved the receiver to left field," Zane said. "I was able to copy the files without anybody realizing it. We got lucky."

Preston grinned. *"Nicely done. And what about your teammates? Any thoughts?"*

"If we are following the logic that the suspect has played in all the games, and has little to no family come around, then we're down to Amber Hyatt, Dorian Delini, and Erik Olsson."

"We?" Preston asked.

Zane panicked a half second before recovering. "As in 'you and me.'"

Preston studied Zane, then began taking notes. *"Well, that's the logic before us. So Amber, Dorian, and Erik. Now, the file. Can you show me the chip?"*

Zane took his cleats out of his bag and popped out the card. "Here she is."

"Can you take out the case I left you?"

Zane went to his sock drawer and fetched the black box Preston had told him not to lose. "Okay, got it."

"Open it up," Preston instructed. *"The micro SD card for your cleats goes in the adapter."*

Zane followed along.

"The adapter goes into the orange card reader," Preston continued. *"That decrypts it and makes it secure. That's pretty much it. Just plug the card reader into a USB port on your computer."*

"Okay, done," Zane said.

"Good. I got it from here."

Zane watched the screen with anticipation. And then it went black.

"Preston?"

"Sorry, still here. I have to darken your screen while I handle this file. Sorry. It's classified."

"I got it for you!"

"Sorry," Preston said. *"I'll be done in a few minutes and tell you everything I can."*

Zane sat there staring at the black screen, stewing. "Did you see the file yet?"

The screen flickered back to life. Preston wasn't happy. *"They've got the list of actual identities."*

"Oh, no."

"Now, they can't read it or match it up with the code-names unless they hack in again and steal the digital decoder key. We're still okay."

"How is this okay? And you didn't answer my question earlier. We need to end this. Like now. We're out of time. Amber, Dorian, Erik. Arrest all three. Dig up the receiver. Why are we still taking this chance when my mom's life is at stake?"

"Things have changed," Preston said. *"There's more going on here than you know."*

"What then? What's going on?"

"I can't tell you everything. I'm sorry. You're going to have to trust me."

"Here's what I'm going to do," Zane said. "I'm going back to the field right now and taking that receiver or hackbox or whatever you wanna call it so the spy can't get the decoder key."

"Don't cross me. I'd have you stopped before you got there. Unless the spy got to you first, then who knows what would happen. We're on the same side, believe it or not. Countless lives are counting on you, and I can't let you blow it."

Zane felt trapped. "At what point is this over?"

"You have to figure out—for sure—who we go after. If we go after the wrong kid, the real spy will get alarmed and be long gone. You have a chance to help your country. You could be a hero here. And we have three games to work with, so we have to try. This could be huge."

"We don't have three games to work with," Zane said.

"What are you talking about? I have your schedule right in front of me."

Zane slammed his hands on the table. "You're reading it wrong. That schedule shows the length of the entire season, playoffs included."

"What?"

"We barely made it into the playoffs," Zane said. "Coming up we have the quarterfinals Thursday, semifinals Friday, then the championship Saturday. Only if we keep winning though. If we lose in the quarterfinals, we're done."

"No!" Preston shouted. His demeanor cracked. Zane saw the older man stand up from his computer and start pacing around. *"That's not the information I had. This is bad. This is bad."*

"Now do you see?" Zane asked. "I don't know what else you aren't telling me, but we're out of time."

"No, we're not. We can't end this. I wish we could, but we can't. You don't understand. I need more information. If the season ends, this whole thing is over. The games are the cover. They have to continue. Your mission just got more important than you realize."

"Well, at least we have a game Thursday."

Preston sat back down and leaned in close. His eyes were piercing through the screen. *"I can't say this any more clearly. If you haven't completed your mission by the end of the game Thursday, you can NOT let the season end. You either bring me the name of the spy and a fresh download right after the game Thursday, or win the game so you have another shot to do it in the semifinals. The security of this country and your family's future literally depends on you, Zane. Do you understand?"*

Zane didn't respond. What choice did he have?

"Zane?" Preston repeated, calming down.

"Yeah, I'm listening," Zane said, staring off into space. He was already thinking of creative ways to go download the file. Singling out either Amber, Dorian, or Erik would be harder. Thank God for Teddy. Would his plan actually work?

CHAPTER 17

"WHAT IF SHE doesn't go for it?" Teddy asked.

"She will," Zane said. "How could she not?"

The teammates were walking to Regal View Park for Wednesday morning's practice.

"Well, for one, he's better looking than me," Teddy said. "And cooler."

"I can't argue with that. But it's a free show we're talking about."

"Free for her. For me they were one eighty—each. That's the rest of my Bar Mitzvah money right there. Poof. Gone. These tickets are so expensive. Now you know why my dad trusts me to go alone with her."

"Because he doesn't want to spend a hundred and eighty dollars of his money to chaperone?" Zane guessed.

"Bingo."

"Funny how your parents suddenly trust you when it saves them money," Zane said.

Teddy kicked a crumpled Coke can in his path. "You

know there's no way she's the spy. It's okay for me to actually *want* her to say 'yes' since she's a normal kid. Who's abnormally hot."

"I hope you're right," Zane said.

"I am right. Think about it. If I'm another country and am going to place an undercover spy on a baseball team, I would want the spy to blend in with the other kids. Sending a girl to play on a team of all boys isn't exactly blending in."

"Good point," Zane said, mulling it over. "But remember, this might not be coming from another country."

"Yeah, but it might," Teddy said. "Either way, she's not exactly the most athletic person around. So, do we cross her off the list?"

"Probably. If you get her to go tonight, you can have all the time you need to find out for sure."

"And we mess up Dorian's date," Teddy said, grinning. "But what if she still wants to go with Dorian tonight instead of go to the concert?"

"We'll figure something out," Zane said.

They got to the field. Dorian and Amber were already there, playing catch.

Teddy, to his credit, spoke up. "Hi, Amber."

"Hey," she said back.

Dorian gave Teddy a look.

Teddy pretended not to notice.

"Playoff time!" Rudy yelled, plopping a bucket of balls on home plate.

All the players started hooting and hollering.

"Never had a doubt, guys," he said. "Positions. Same as yesterday."

The players all jogged to their spots and began fielding balls from their coach. Rudy's large gut didn't stop him from employing his textbook swing, hitting perfectly placed grounders and pop flies. Over the next hour, the coaches ran the Renegades through the regular drills while classic rock played out of a wireless speaker on the ground. When it was over, the players were playing catch with each other and milling around the dugout.

"Dorian," Rudy said. "I need you to do some extra work with Sammy, sharpen things up. Thirty pitches."

"Coach, I'm good."

Rudy looked back at him and shook his head. "Dorian, I'm telling you to pitch."

"Whatever."

Rudy was on him in a flash. "'Whatever?' Do *not* 'whatever' me. Around the field. Three times."

The team got quiet and stared at Rudy and the player suddenly challenging his authority.

Dorian's defiant expression didn't change, but he was smart enough to say the right words. "Sorry, coach." He got up and started jogging down the right field line.

Rudy looked at the players. "You guys can joke around all you want. But it is never okay to be disrespectful. Stretch it out."

Teddy was off to the side with Amber. It was as good a chance as he was going to get. Dorian was running his laps. Zane hung nearby, ready to eavesdrop as soon as Teddy made his move. Teddy stood there for a moment, unsure how to begin. Zane felt even more nervous than his friend. Asking a girl out really was impossible. How did Dorian make it look so easy?

"Hey, uh, Amber?" Teddy said.

"Nice plays out there, Rempke," she said.

"Thanks."

Amber waited for him to say something else. Teddy stood there awkwardly. Zane couldn't bear to watch. *Do it!* he thought to himself.

Amber turned to leave. "I'm gonna—"

"Say," Teddy interrupted. "I have two tickets to Chandler DeNario tonight."

"Sweet," she said.

Teddy finally spit it out. "Would you, uh... like to go with me?"

"Wow. That's awesome. Aren't those tickets like two hundred dollars?"

Teddy, empowered by her enthusiasm, rediscovered his ability to talk. "Yeah, my dad got them through work. It'll be amazing. For reals. Come with me."

Dorian ran past the dugout and headed down the right field line again. His eyes were burning a hole through Teddy as he started his second lap.

"Except I kind of already have plans with Dorian," Amber said. "Sorry. Go with Zane. You guys'll have a blast."

"For sure. That's what I was going to do." Teddy stood there, dejected.

The scene was hard for Zane to watch. He looked around, thinking. He counted the players on the field and did some quick math in his head.

This better be worth it, he thought. He jogged over to the dugout, glanced to see if Rudy was watching, then powered on his phone. He checked the site to see if it was even an option. It was.

"Teddy," Zane called.

Teddy was eager for any excuse to leave Amber. He came over and sat next to Zane. He held his hand up sideways and pretended it was a plane crashing to the ground. "*Earrrrrrpuhoosh.* Crashed and burned. She's keeping her plans with Dorian. But at least I asked. I did it. I asked a girl on a date."

"I know, I saw," Zane said. "You did great. You know how I said we'd think of something?"

"Yeah, what?"

"Well, here's my 'something.'"

Teddy looked at the phone. "Are you crazy? Why would you do that?"

"If *everybody* goes tonight, then she'll still be with Dorian. So, she won't technically be breaking her date with him. And you get to be there as well. You could sit on the other side of her. Or at least talk to her a little."

"It's not exactly how I pictured it—at all."

"Better than nothing," said Zane, talking fast. "You get to talk to her. She won't be alone with Dorian. We can do some scouting on Amber, Dorian, and Erik. Not to mention go rock out at the best concert we'll probably ever see. You're already stuck going. You bought the tickets. Might as well go with everybody, instead of going with me and stewing over the fact that Amber is somewhere else, alone with Dorian."

"How are you going to pay for all those extra tickets?"

Zane smiled big.

"That's right!" Teddy shouted. "The Visa cards."

"Keep it down," Zane said, looking around, still smiling. "And yes."

"Oh, right. Sorry. You are really gonna spend all that money on this?"

"I've got close to two grand. I've barely touched it. Why not do something awesome with it?"

"Wow," Teddy said. "Thanks. That's so cool. It would have been cooler if you thought of this before I paid three hundred sixty dollars of my own money."

Zane looked at Teddy and threw up his hands.

"Kidding!" Teddy said.

"But it's a good point," Zane said.

"Preston will let you go?"

"I think, since it's for the mission," Zane said. "But honestly, he's been coming in so late he won't even know about it until after we've left. Heck, by the time he gets home, I'll probably be back in bed. He'll never know. Unless the agents are watching me and make me leave or something. But either way, better to ask for forgiveness instead of permission."

"But how are you going to explain this to the team? And what about parents?"

"Say your dad got more tickets," Zane said. "A *lot* more."

"What about parents?" Teddy repeated. "The other parents are going to want to know an adult is there." Teddy quickly took out his phone and tapped the screen a few times. He looked at Zane and crossed his fingers.

CHAPTER 18

THE BOYS PACKED up their gear and started to do their finishing stretches before Rudy dismissed them.

"Coach?" Teddy asked. "Do you mind if I make an announcement before everybody leaves?"

"Go ahead."

Dorian finished his third lap and put his hands up on his head. He headed for the dugout, breathing hard. Teddy walked quickly over to Amber before Dorian was within earshot.

"Hey, so my dad actually has a ton of tickets for to-night," Teddy said. "I'm gonna invite the whole team."

"Seriously?" she asked.

"You and Dorian can come together."

She bit her lower lip. "Hmmm."

Rudy interrupted the exchange. "Listen up. I don't know about you guys, but I'm pretty excited for the quar-terfinals tomorrow. We win tomorrow and the next one, then this team is playing for a title. Everybody meet at

Falcon at four fifteen. No. Better make it four o'clock. Teddy, you got something?"

The players all turned and looked at Teddy.

"Yeah," he said nervously. He cleared his throat. "So, sorry this is last minute. But my dad told me that he has free tickets to the Chandler DeNario concert tonight. We have enough to take the whole team."

The team gasped. Ricky's giant bubble popped. "No way!" he shouted, wiping the gum off his face.

"Is this a joke?" Yuri asked.

"He got them through work. They're all on his phone. He can transfer them to you digitally. All you have to do is let us know if you are coming, and then get dropped off at six forty-five by the statue in front of the main entrance. My dad and I will meet everyone there. So, get my number before you leave. I have to know within the next hour or so if you're coming. Your parents can call my dad to confirm it all."

Everybody cheered. Everybody except Dorian, who never stopped staring at Teddy. Teddy ignored him and turned to Amber. "You guys have to come," he said. "Chandler DeNario!"

"Yeah, you're totally right," she said. Amber walked over to Dorian.

"Our date just got a lot more interesting," Amber said.

Dorian finally smiled, but his eyes never left Teddy. "Yes, it did," he said.

Teddy gave out his and his dad's cell phone numbers. The teammates made the arrangements and started to head their separate ways. Teddy and Zane sat on the curb, pretending to wait for a ride. In reality, they wanted to see who was coming to pick up Amber, Dorian, and Erik. Dorian rode away with Erik, and somehow they lost track of Amber on the other side of the field.

"Teddy!" The boys turned around to see Sammy Logan running up. "I heard Dorian talking to Erik. He said something like, 'I'm gonna kill him.' I think he wants to try something tonight at the concert. He's totally pissed."

"He didn't say that," Zane said. "Teddy's giving him a ticket to the concert. Why would he try that?"

Teddy put both hands on his head and leaned forward. "You know why."

"He's mad all the time," Sammy said. "And Erik does whatever he says."

"Whatever," Zane said. "Dorian's full of it."

Sammy's mom pulled up, and he headed for the car. "Only trying to help."

"Gee, thanks," Teddy said.

"See you guys tonight. Thanks again for the tickets. I got your back, Teddy!"

"See you there," Teddy said.

Teddy and Zane were the last ones left. They got up and started heading home on foot.

"Great idea, Zane," Teddy said. "He's gonna kill me! Dorian Delini is gonna kill me."

"Dude, he's all talk."

"He's the strongest, toughest kid on the team. Who knows what's going on in his head?"

"It doesn't matter. Your dad is going to be right there. Nobody is going to kill anybody."

"Getting punched by two teammates in the same week? That's gotta be a record, right?"

The man had been waiting ahead in the parked car, engine running. He poked his head out at the exact wrong time. When his eyes met Zane's, he ducked his head back in the car.

Zane tensed.

"Zane?" Teddy asked.

"Shorty," he whispered to Teddy.

Shorty revved the engine.

"Run!" Zane shouted.

Zane spun around and started to sprint back to the practice field. Teddy followed. They heard the screech of tires peeling away on the pavement. Zane looked back over his shoulder in between steps. The car was gone.

CHAPTER 19

"IT'S RINGING," ZANE said, crouching low and catching his breath.

The creek behind Regal View Park provided a little cover but not as much as Zane and Teddy would have hoped. Still, it was better than standing out in the open.

"He didn't chase us." Teddy was oddly calm for a guy laying down against a fallen tree. "Why didn't he chase us? And how does a homeless guy get a car?"

The ringing continued.

"Maybe he lives in the car," Zane said. "But that's not the point. Where are the agents that are supposed to be watching me?"

Just when Zane thought the call would go to voice-mail, Preston finally answered. *"Anything to report?"*

"Yes, Shorty's back. He was waiting outside our practice. He saw me and revved his engine. We turned and ran, but I think he drove away."

"You said he drove away?" Preston asked.

"Yes."

"Where are you? Are you safe?"

"Hiding in a creek. I don't know. I think he's gone. What do we do?"

"First, I have to tell you something. This is the second straight conversation you said the word 'we.'"

Uh-oh.

"Who's 'we?'" Preston asked.

Zane looked at Teddy, who shrugged. Zane took a deep breath and continued. "Uh... my friend Teddy. He was with me when I saw Shorty. I freaked out, and we both ran."

"How would he know to run?"

"You don't understand," Zane said, looking at Teddy. "I needed help the other day when Shorty was after me the first time. I had to hide somewhere, and Teddy's house was a minute away. I know Teddy isn't the spy, so I asked for help. I couldn't help it. You have to believe me."

"I don't 'have' to do anything. How do you know Teddy isn't the spy? He was on the list you gave me."

"No he wasn't."

"He was the 'T.' Why didn't you finish writing his name?"

"Okay, he is new on the team this year, but I think he missed one of the earlier games that the hacker was active. I didn't realize it until later."

"You 'think' he missed a game?"

"I know he did. And I could tell by the way he reacted when I went to his house. And he's *Teddy*. If you knew him, you'd know what I mean."

Zane leaned away from the phone and said, "No offense, Teddy."

"None taken," Teddy said.

"He's been helping us out," Zane continued. "Why would he do that?"

"To lead you down the wrong path perhaps?" Preston said. *"To keep you off balance? Do you realize how incredibly awful this could be?"*

"He's not the spy," Zane said.

"Are you willing to risk your life on that?" Preston asked. *"Does he know everything?"*

"He's not the spy," Zane said again, looking at Teddy a few feet away. Teddy couldn't hear everything Preston was saying but could get the gist of it.

"Has he told anyone?" Preston asked.

"Not even his dad," Zane said. "He understands not to. He knows how serious it is."

"I could have you both arrested," Preston said. *"In fact, I should. At this point, it would be safer that way."*

"You need me." Zane stayed low and took a step away from Teddy, making it harder for his friend to follow along.

"Then I'll arrest Teddy."

"If you do that, I'll tell the whole team that Teddy was arrested for being a spy," Zane said. "Then the real spy will be tipped off, grab their receiver, and be gone."

"Then what?" asked Preston. *"The hacker bolts. Maybe he gets the decoder key first. All U.S. identities are compromised, and you and your mom lose everything, remember? Start packing. You guys will need to vanish into hiding. Unless you're killed first. Sounds like fun, right? You need this mission to work even more than I do."*

"Okay!" Zane regretted raising his volume. He looked

around to make sure Shorty hadn't circled back and followed them to the creek.

"Zane?" Teddy whispered. "What's going on?"

Zane held up a finger.

Preston spoke. *"Look, I'm sorry I threatened Teddy. But just because you trust him doesn't mean I have to. I am not going to arrest him. You're right. That doesn't make sense. Chances are you are correct. We don't have what we need yet, so we have to proceed as is. But I don't like this. Even if he isn't the spy, he might talk about the mission."*

"I'm sorry, too. He won't talk, he gets it. You have to believe me, I really didn't have any other choice at the time. You weren't there. You're trusting me to do this job. I know he's not the spy. I also know I need his help. Your agents weren't there when I needed them. And where are they now? Shorty's here! We saw him, and he drove away. Teddy and I are crouching down in a muddy creek."

"I know you're scared, but let's calm down. It doesn't sound like you're in trouble. Think about it. All that happened was that a guy saw you and drove away."

"He owns a gun. What if he's coming back for me?"

"Why would he?" Preston asked. *"It sounds like you freaked this 'Shorty' whacko out. He's avoiding you for fear of being arrested. I'm certain that's why he drove away. And anybody can carry a gun these days. He never even showed it to you. But if it makes you feel better, my agents are nearby. They must have not called me or made a move because they never saw any danger. Never break cover if you don't have to."*

"So, they're out there right now?" Zane asked.

"Three agents are stationed at various spots on your route

home. I'll put them on high alert right now. You're fine. Get out of that creek and head home, both of you. Just be careful."

Teddy kept looking at Zane, waiting. Zane stood up and gave him a thumbs up. Teddy relaxed and straightened up, too, brushing sticks and burrs from his baseball pants.

"Okay," Zane said. "I'm going to Teddy's for a while. I don't want to be alone. I'll be careful."

"Keep a close eye on him, too," Preston said. *"Remind him every minute how crucial it is to keep his mouth shut. And from now on, no more lies. You tell me everything. Eh-ve-ry-thing."*

"I will."

"What time is the game tomorrow?" Preston asked.

"Five."

"You remember what you need to do?"

"Trust me, I know," Zane said. "Make a download and figure out—for sure—who the spy is. And if I can't do those things, win the game to buy us another chance in the semifinals."

"Very good. Are we still looking at only Erik, Dorian, and Amber?"

"Amber's looking less likely," Zane said. "If our latest theory turns out to be true, we could be down to Erik and Dorian."

"I believe in you." Preston sounded like a different person than the one who had threatened to arrest Zane and Teddy moments earlier. *"I know you can do this. Mainly because you have no choice."*

"I know, I know," Zane said, trying not to think about how big tomorrow really was.

"Nervous and confident at the same time, I like that," Preston said. *"Reminds me of someone."*

"Who?"

Preston paused. *"Not important. Anyways, I know you don't want to be alone, but I'm stuck at the CRU until very, very late. I'm sorry I can't be there tonight when you get back from Teddy's. You gonna be okay?"*

"I'll be fine," Zane said.

"Okay, then," Preston said. *"Just do me a favor?"*

"What?"

"Try to lay low until this whole thing is over."

Zane looked at Teddy and smiled.

"Of course."

CHAPTER 20

MR. REMPKE PULLED out of the garage and drove off into the night with Teddy in the front and Zane in the back.

"Thanks again, pops," Teddy said. "I know you don't exactly feel like a million bucks."

Mr. Rempke smiled. "I do tonight."

Zane thought of his mom. Wasn't she worried about him? Shouldn't she break the rules and call him? This thing was getting scary. Where would they be in a week? Would they even be together?

"Thanks, Mister Rempke," Zane said.

"I owe you the thank you," he said. "Your mom at least. That is so great that she got all these tickets. I'm sorry she couldn't come with us."

"Yeah. Me, too. Work comes first. That's what she always says."

As the car drove on, Zane braced for the phone call. He guessed Preston's undercover agents would have seen him leave the Rempke house, relayed the info, and Preston would have reacted. Zane was prepared to tell Mr. Rempke something came up, and he would have to be dropped off back at home. Except the call never came. They were almost to the concert, and the phone had not made a beep.

Teddy looked back at Zane and gave a reassuring nod. Either the agents saw Zane leave with the Rempkes and didn't care, or they missed it altogether. Either way, Zane figured he could relax for the time being. If Preston got mad later, Zane would simply tell him the truth—mission business, and he didn't want Preston to interfere.

While Teddy and his dad goofed around up front with the radio, Zane was busy staring out the backseat windows. Every time he saw a black car that looked like Shorty's, he ducked lower in his seat, tensing up until he could see the driver.

Mr. Rempke smacked the top of the wheel with his palm. "Here!" he announced.

"Sweet," Teddy said.

"What's the big deal about this CBM guy, anyway?" Mr. Rempke asked.

"Dad."

"CDM? No. CDN? CDN."

"Please, don't embarrass me?"

"Right," he said. "Sit there silently."

"Works for me," Teddy said. "And it's CDN. Chandler DeNario."

They parked the car and walked to the ticket window. Dorian and Amber were already there, standing around, not sure how to act. Amber had on ripped jeans, a black leather jacket, and the perfect amount of makeup.

"Dang," Teddy said to Zane as they approached. "She could be a backup dancer."

"Just be cool," Zane whispered.

"Hi, guys," Teddy said, anxious to see how Dorian would handle it.

Dorian showed a warm, relaxed smile and stuck out his hand. "There they are," Dorian said, laying on the charm. "Nice to meet you, Mr. Rempke. I'm Dorian."

"I'm Amber."

Mr. Rempke shook their hands. "Nice to finally meet you guys. It's been fun watching you. Teddy is lucky to have such great teammates."

"It's been great getting to know Teddy," Dorian said. "He's a great ballplayer, too."

Zane had to stop himself from rolling his eyes.

"And thank you for these tickets," Amber added.

"Tickets?" Mr. Rempke asked.

"You're welcome," Teddy said quickly. "We couldn't let them go to waste."

Mr. Rempke started to say something, but Zane interrupted. "Anybody else here?"

"Not yet," Dorian said.

Mr. Rempke looked over his shoulder to see Erik and his mom approaching.

Teddy got Amber's attention. "You look really nice."

"Thanks, Rempke," Amber said.

Dorian smiled big at Teddy, a little too big.

"What?" Amber broke up the awkward moment.

Erik, Ricky, Yuri, and Sammy eventually showed up, completing their group. Mateo and the injured Braxton weren't coming. The Atwater twins were already in the building, enjoying the front row seats their father got them a month ago. Once assembled, they all began the walk to their seats.

"You boys want to tell me what's going on now?" Mr. Rempke said to Zane and Teddy.

"Zane is embarrassed that his mom was able to get all those tickets," Teddy whispered.

"Yeah, sorry," Zane said. "I didn't want people making a big deal about it. I thought it would be okay if we said you guys got the tickets through your work or something. I know it's weird, sorry."

"I'm a plumber. Who hasn't worked in months."

Teddy laughed. "Yeah, but they don't know that."

Mr. Rempke shrugged. "If that's what you guys want."

Teddy and Zane made eye contact, satisfied that another last-second lie got the job done.

They went up, up, up to the top of the arena. Zane and Teddy were at the rear of the group with the slow-moving Mr. Rempke.

"Hey," Zane whispered. "You have to get up there next to her by the time we get to our section. I don't care how many looks Dorian gives you, make sure you sit with her. That's the whole reason we're here—for you *and* for me."

"Agreed." Teddy walked ahead of his dad and closed the gap between him and Amber. When they got to their seats, Teddy scooted ahead of Ricky in the line so he could be right behind Amber. The group had two rows of seats. Erik walked in to the first row, followed by Dorian, Amber, then Teddy. Teddy sat down next to her, accomplishing his mission. Ricky was about to sit in the next seat after Teddy but then realized it was on the aisle.

"Oh, Mister Rempke, you probably want to sit next to Teddy," Ricky said.

"Thanks, if you don't mind," he said.

Mr. Rempke sat down next to his son. Ricky went to the next row up and walked down to his seat, followed by Yuri, Sammy, and lastly Zane. Zane was directly behind Teddy, a perfect position to monitor the situation.

The building was buzzing with excitement as everyone waited for the show to start. Zane tried to act interested as he scanned the crowd for Shorty, then scanned for exits. The background music was getting louder, but conversation was still possible. Dorian was leaning to his left, talking to Erik in a low voice. Teddy saw his opening.

"Do your mom and dad like CDN as much as you do?" Teddy asked Amber.

"Uh-yeah, no," she said. "Anything made after 1990 is a no-go in our house."

Zane leaned forward so he could hear better.

Teddy kept the conversation with Amber going. "Can I ask you something?" he asked.

"Lemme guess," she said. "Why am I playing baseball instead of softball?"

"Sorry," Teddy said. "I didn't want it to sound like I don't want you on the team. But, yeah. Why?"

"No, it's fine. Everybody wants to know. I was playing softball before we moved. I should be playing softball."

"So…?"

"This league we are in now is great," she said. "The Renegades are a perfect fit for me. It's not a travel or club team. Less money. Less pressure."

"Yeah, less pressure," Teddy said.

Amber continued. "All I want is a place to come and play two or three times a week without having to ask my parents to pay a fortune and drive two hours each way every Saturday."

"So, at this age it's all club on the softball side?" Teddy asked.

"Mostly," she said. "Last year in Miami, I did club for the first time, and it was overwhelming. So, when we moved here, my parents flat out said they didn't want to go through another summer like that, especially since my parents work so much. There's rec leagues here, but from what I heard, they're pretty weak. And since my dad ruled out club, I was stuck. Next spring and summer I won't have this problem. I'll be playing high school softball hopefully. But this is kind of an 'in between' year for me."

"Why not just play in the lesser softball league? Again, not that I don't want you here."

"Ha. Relax, Rempke." She patted him on the knee. "I needed a challenge. My mom said I should go beat up on the boys. My dad told me I shouldn't do it. He was totally against it actually. But that just made me want to play on the Renegades even more."

"What's your dad do?" Teddy asked.

"Annoys me," she said.

"No, I mean his job."

"Who cares about my dad's job?" Amber laughed.

Dorian, seated on Amber's left, said something that made her giggle. Teddy leaned forward, straining to hear over the increasing noise. Once the music started going full blast, his chance to chat would be over. He tried to jump back in.

"How long have you guys lived in D.C.?" Teddy asked.

"Hey!" said a loud voice. It was Erik shouting from Dorian's other side. "Why don't you leave them alone?"

Teddy turned red. "Okay," he said. "Good idea."

Dorian said something to Erik.

Erik shook his head. "They're on a date, remember?"

Dorian elbowed Erik in the arm. Mr. Rempke was looking at his phone, completely unaware of the drama.

Now Amber was red. The background music got louder. The lights dimmed, and everybody cheered.

"What's Erik's problem?" Zane asked Sammy.

"I think he's trying to get Teddy to shut up so Dorian can have more time with Amber," he said.

"Yeah, but how is it Erik's problem?" Zane asked.

"I don't know. Does it matter? Just avoid those guys. Avoid them like the plague. But we do have a problem. Like I told you, Dorian's gonna try something with Teddy."

"No way," Zane said. "His dad's right here."

"Not for long," Sammy said. "Check it out." Teddy's dad was standing up to leave. He looked a bit wobbly.

"I need to use the bathroom," Mr. Rempke said, still oblivious to the tension. "Hey, everybody. I'll be back in ten with some caffeine."

"Are you sure you can do all the walking?" Teddy asked. "Maybe you should sit for a bit."

"I'm fine. I got it."

Teddy looked concerned.

"Get out of here with that look," Mr. Rempke said. "I'm fine, don't worry. Have fun." He motioned to Amber as he left. Teddy looked at Amber to make sure she didn't notice. He slunk into his seat again.

As Mr. Rempke left, Sammy and Zane exchanged an uneasy glance through the dimly lit space. They could hear Erik and Dorian laughing about something.

"It's fine," Zane said to Sammy. "As long as Amber is here, Dorian will be an angel."

"Hey, Amber," Erik yelled over the music. "Teddy thinks you're hot!"

Teddy sat there embarrassed, staring at the floor.

"Ugh," Amber said. She stood up and glared at Erik. "I think I'm going to check on Mister Rempke." She stepped across Teddy and vanished down the stairs.

The lights dimmed even further. The place was bubbling over with excitement. Erik and Dorian stood up, then turned to face Teddy.

CHAPTER 21

TEDDY STOOD UP. Zane watched to see if he was going to turn right and run down the stairs toward his dad, or turn to his left and face his enemies.

Teddy took a breath and turned to his left. He narrowed his eyes. "What?"

"You," Dorian said, taking a step closer. "The only reason you did all this was so you could mess up my date with Amber."

All the other boys leaned in. Teddy didn't flinch. Maybe it was the energy of the concert, maybe it was because he doubted Dorian would do anything with Teddy's dad around. Whatever it was, Teddy stood his ground.

"Whatever," Teddy said. "We got all these tickets and invited everybody. You should be thanking me."

"He should be fighting you," Erik yelled over the noise. "For realsssss. Isn't that your lame saying?"

"C'mon!" Zane yelled from the back row. "We're teammates, remember? What are you guys going to do?

Hit a guy who brought you to a concert along with his cancer-stricken father? That would look great."

Dorian's face said it all. He knew Zane was right. "I had to say something," Dorian said. "It wasn't cool, and you know it. You owe me an apology." Dorian poked his finger hard into Teddy's chest.

Teddy knocked away his hand. "Get your hands off me. I didn't do anything wrong. You owe me an apology for threatening me and ruining tonight. And you and Erik and Braxton have been horrible all season. You guys suck the fun out of baseball. I'm sick of it."

"I didn't threaten you," Dorian said. "And if I put my hands on you, you'd know it. I'm just mad."

"Over nothing," Teddy said. "Erik, get off my case."

"*Your* case?" Erik said, smirking.

"Okay, that's enough!" Sammy yelled. "Can we all puh-leeze chill and enjoy the concert?"

"Yeah, all this over Amber?" Ricky said, chiming in. "Dorian, bro, you hate Amber."

The boys laughed.

"What are you talking about, Ricky?" Dorian said. He was about to say something else but then saw Amber on her way back to the seats.

"Forget it." Dorian sat down, defeated. Teddy stood there proudly. Not only had he faced Dorian, but his teammates had backed him up. Amber returned. Zane got the impression she hadn't gone far.

"Are you guys done?" she said. "You're being weird."

"It's fine," Dorian said.

Erik remained quiet but was grinning like he was the only one that knew the answer to a riddle. Amber slid past Teddy toward her seat between him and Dorian. She gave Teddy a wink. Teddy looked at Dorian, who definitely noticed the wink.

"*WHAT'S UP D.C.?!*" boomed the speakers. The dark arena suddenly glowed as torches shot flames thirty feet into the air. Even from the upper deck of the arena, Zane could feel the fire's heat on his face. A laser light show began, synched up to the beat of the music. The crowd went wild.

"*C-D-N! C-D-N! C-D-N!*"

The whole team chanted along, even Dorian and Erik. Zane started to relax a little.

The fire disappeared, and a giant circular platform rose up from the ground where the fire had been moments before. On it, Chandler DeNario, already belting out his first song. The crowd cheered even louder and began to sing along. Teddy's dad returned with two trays worth of drinks.

"What'd I miss?" he shouted to his son.

"Everything!" Teddy shouted back.

Teddy looked back at Zane, who gave him a nod. Amber was dancing away, with Dorian on her left and Teddy on her right. The girl knew how to lighten the mood.

Zane was jumping around with his teammates, but his mind was not in the moment, not by a longshot. He focused on why he was there—information. The season might end tomorrow, and he still couldn't say which of his remaining suspects was actually a spy on the verge of stealing explosive government secrets. Had he learned anything tonight? Amber's backstory sure sounded legit. Dorian was such a wild card, and Erik was pure aggression. Which one of his teammates was an impostor? He better figure it out fast—or win.

He looked over at Mr. Rempke. The guy was battling his own fight but was having a blast. Zane's mind wandered to his mom again. What risks did she face? What about himself? If he failed, they would have to leave town without saying goodbye to anybody and go into hiding.

Think, Zane! he said to nobody.

Despite all the pressure, he finally allowed himself a moment to appreciate how incredible the concert was. Zane had no idea a show like this would have so many special effects and giant screens. It was sensory overload, definitely worth every government dollar.

When it ended, Zane saw a camaraderie amongst his teammates that was the best it had been all summer— with the exception of Erik and Dorian. The rest of the guys didn't seem so intimidated by them anymore. Maybe this group could come together after all and win another game. Zane would have to be at his absolute best tomorrow, physically and mentally. His life literally depended on it.

"Best show ever!" Ricky yelled, smacking on his gum.

"He played every hit," Yuri said. "I don't have to go to another concert ever again. My first one will never be topped." They all agreed.

The house lights slowly came on. Everybody started to cram together as they exited down the stairs. It was hard to see. Erik was clutching his cup of soda filled with leftover ice.

"Hey, Dorian," he sneered. "I got you, man."

"Dude, don't," Dorian said.

Erik let a few teammates pass him until Teddy was directly behind him. Erik emptied the ice on the step and continued down. Teddy wasn't paying attention but, fortunately, stepped right over the ice and onto the next step below. Zane, who was behind Teddy, was not so lucky. His foot landed and immediately gave out. His butt dropped to the ground like a sack of rocks. He stuck out his left hand to brace his fall but ended up getting his hand caught between his butt and the corner of the concrete step. Zane screamed, wincing in pain.

"You all right?" Teddy asked.

His hand was searing. He breathed in hard through his nostrils, trying to control the sensation. "No… something's wrong," he gasped. "It's bad. There's… ice on the step."

Traffic on the stairs behind them was backing up. Sammy and Yuri bent down to pick Zane up. Zane used his foot to brush away the ice so nobody else would slip. Everyone continued down the steps. When they exited the concourse and eventually got outside, Mr. Rempke wanted to take a look. Zane tried to play it cool. He had calmed down a little, but it wasn't easy.

"It looks swollen," Mr. Rempke said. "Let's call your mom, just in case."

"It's really not that bad," Zane lied. "I can ice it when I get home."

"You okay?" Amber asked.

"I'll be fine."

Mr. Rempke took a call from one of the parents and started looking around the street.

"Hey, Zane," Erik said. "You really should be more careful where you step." Erik smiled, then looked at

Dorian for a laugh. Dorian looked at the ground silently, and took a subtle half step away from Erik.

"What?" Erik asked.

"Oh, hey, I see you," Mr. Rempke said into the phone. "I'll send them over. Yeah. You bet. They were great."

Several of the parents were parked on the curb across the street, waiting.

"Thanks Mister Rempke," Dorian said. He pointed. "That's us over there."

"Mine, too," Erik said.

"Anybody else?" Mr. Rempke asked.

"Yup," Yuri said. "Thank you, sir. It was great."

Mr. Rempke, Zane, and Teddy waited near the ticket window with Sammy and Ricky, whose parents had not arrived yet. Zane watched as Dorian and Amber, along with Erik and Yuri, crossed the street and got in their respective cars.

Dorian opened the back door for Amber, who smiled and said something as she got in. Zane could see Dorian's mom in front. He seemed to be getting along with her this time. She waved at Mr. Rempke as she drove off. Mr. Rempke waved back.

Then Zane noticed it. Some sort of official looking sticker on the Delini's windshield. It contained a symbol of a blue and white striped flag with a white cross in the upper left.

"Teddy, look at Dorian's windshield," Zane said quietly.

"What?" Teddy said back, making sure Sammy and Ricky weren't paying attention.

Zane gave Teddy an eager look, but Teddy just shrugged back apologetically.

Once all their teammates had been picked up, Zane and Teddy followed Mr. Rempke to the parking garage.

"I'll have to send your parents some pictures," Mr. Rempke said as they got to the car. "I got some good ones. That was some night."

"Sure was," Zane said, blocking out the pain radiating from his hand.

"You okay?" asked Mr. Rempke.

"Yup, just tired." Zane tried to get in the car, but his hand hurt too bad to open the door.

CHAPTER 22

THE NEXT DAY, Mr. Rempke felt well enough to give the boys a ride to Falcon Field for their quarterfinal playoff game against the Vipers.

"I'll be back by the third or fourth, depending on how long this appointment takes," he said.

Teddy and Zane thanked him, and Mr. Rempke drove off. Zane started to wave but then tucked his left hand back down, grimacing.

"You okay?" Teddy asked.

"No. I iced it all last night and took Ibuprofen around the clock. But it still hurts to open and shut."

"How are you going to play? You can't even play catch."

"I don't have a choice. I have to be in the field."

"Did you tell Preston?"

"No," Zane said. "By the time he got home it was almost midnight. I was already in bed. I don't even think he knows we went to the concert. And I wasn't about to bring it up."

"Did he tuck you in at least?" Teddy asked.

"It's not funny. But we did talk. Get this. He said he didn't need to stay the night anymore. He'd been getting home so late each night, and since we're almost done with the mission, he didn't see the point. He asked me if I'm okay with it, which I am. He'll keep calling me a bunch and come over when he needs to. Like after we win this game."

"And you can't go home empty-handed, right?"

"I have seven innings to get that download and find out once and for all who the spy is."

"I'll be on the bench," Teddy said, "but I can at least play some more detective. You ever find out about the flag on Dorian's mom's car?"

"Greek," Zane said. "I looked it up."

"Why'd he tell people he's from New York?" Teddy asked. "Is he lying?"

"Don't know," Zane said. "But he told me he spoke Italian. And his mom works in insurance."

"Hmm. That sure is an official looking parking sticker his Mom has for the ol' insurance office."

"Well, we've got about two hours to figure this kid out," Zane said.

"I still say it can't be Amber. I know how smart and capable she is, but I can't let go of my earlier logic. They'd send in a boy to blend in with the other boys. Plus, her story adds up. Which means we're down to Erik or Dorian. You know who my guess is. I'll be watching him the whole game."

"Thanks."

Zane had his new earpiece in and his belt buckle

ready. He looked at his cleats and felt the spike that contained the computer chip. The Renegades were already on the field getting loose. Teddy and Zane dropped their bags in the dugout and greeted Amber and a few of their teammates on the field. Zane noticed Dorian was playing catch with Yuri, not Erik.

Zane walked toward the outfield and heard his first beep. He turned and caught a soft lob from Teddy.

"How is it?" Teddy asked.

"Kills," Zane said, loud enough for only Teddy to hear. He tossed the ball back, grimacing. "But I'm ready. Do it. Like we said."

Teddy threw one hard and high. It sailed over Zane's head and into centerfield toward the receiver. Zane ran underneath it like a wide receiver catching up to a touchdown pass.

BEEP! Beep!

Zane could have caught up to the ball but pulled up early and let it drop. He slowly walked around it.

BEEP! Beep!

Zane froze. The rate of the beeping wasn't increasing as fast as it should. It was basically staying steady. He ignored the baseball he was pretending to retrieve and started to look around. He walked a few feet to his right. Another beep.

BEEP! BEEP! Beep!

The receiver had moved.

Again.

Zane was desperate to at least locate his target. He took another step in that direction and then looked back at the field. Amber was staring at him from second base.

"You lost out there?" she asked.

"I lost something," he said. "A contact."

"You wear contacts?"

"Trying to," Zane said.

"Well, good luck." She turned and threw her ball back to Sammy.

Zane walked back over to the ball in center and used his bare right hand to pick it up. He threw it to Teddy. Teddy acted like he was going to throw it back, and Zane shook his head side to side to wave him off.

"Renegades!" Rudy yelled. "Playoff time."

The players all gathered outside the dugout, hooting and hollering.

"This is fun," their coach said. "We win, we play again. Why not dig in and see if we can get a trophy out of this season, huh?"

Rudy read the lineup card. The Renegades were the home team, beginning the game in the field. Erik was starting at pitcher. He and Cedric were both available to pitch because their previous outing, three days earlier, had been less than fifty pitches. Dorian needed to wait one more game before he could pitch, since he had so many pitches his last time out. The Renegades were counting on Erik to have a solid start. The players took their positions, and the game against the Vipers was about to begin. Teddy remained on the bench. While Erik made his last warmup pitches to Sammy, Dorian was playing first base, throwing ground balls to his fellow infielders. Zane stretched his legs in center and looked over at Amber in right field.

"Ball?" she asked.

"Sorry," Zane said.

"I got one!" Ricky shouted from left.

"Hey, let me catch one on the run," Zane called out. He opened his body toward right center, signaling that's where he wanted to run. Ricky threw a high, deep fly ball.

Zane gave chase. As he crept closer to right, his earpiece started chirping faster.

BEEP! BEEP! Beep!

Zane sprinted toward the gap in right center. He caught up with the ball right as he got to the fence and reached out to make the running catch. At the last second, however, he pulled his glove back and missed it, saving his injured hand.

"That was almost amazing," Amber said. "Almost."

"Then, almost thanks," he said. He flipped her the ball with his right hand. "Here, you throw it in."

BEEP! BEEP! Beep!

Zane tried to act relaxed as he waited to hear the steady beep and swoosh sound, signaling the download.

"Play ball!" yelled the umpire. Warmups were over.

Amber took her spot in right, and looked back at Zane, who was still standing near the outfield fence.

"Yo!" she shouted. "Space cadet. We're starting."

BEEP! BEEP! BEEP! Beep! He hadn't heard a steady tone yet. He wasn't close enough.

"Z!" Rudy shouted from the dugout. "Let's go!"

Zane gave up and trotted to center. The game was underway. The Vipers came up to bat.

In between pitches, he looked back to the spot he had been—the fence in right center. Looming over it was the big electronic scoreboard. It was nice, maybe a bit outdated by today's standards. It came up out of the ground on a series of black, square metal poles. Zane looked back again at the action at home plate and watched the batter take a called third strike.

He looked back to the scoreboard. Stuck to the side of one of the poles was a gray metal box housing the scoreboard's electrical components. Zane looked at it as long as he could from his spot in centerfield. He looked back at the batter just in time to see him swing and miss at Erik's next fastball.

Zane turned back to take another look. That would be the perfect hiding place for the receiver. Plus, the beeps were faster the closer he was to it.

"What?" Amber yelled.

"Just checking the score," Zane said, startled.

"Uh, nothing nothing."

"Oh, yeah!" Zane was embarrassed but comforted by the fact he had at least figured out where the receiver probably was. Now… the spy.

The next batter fouled a line drive right at the Renegades' dugout, hitting the fence in front of Teddy. He fell down, pretending he was struck in the stomach. He grabbed his belly and moaned, cracking up the team.

"He's a character," Zane said, loud enough for Amber to hear in right.

"That's some pretty good acting," she said.

The words hit Zane like a ton of bricks.

"What did you say?" he asked Amber.

"I said Teddy's a good actor. What's with you today?"

Teddy. An actor. The thought swirled around in his head as he watched the at-bat continue.

What if Teddy was acting this whole time?

What if he really wasn't who he said he was?

What if…?

"No way," he said out loud.

"What?" Amber said from right.

Zane pretended not to hear. He could feel goosebumps on his arms. He was replaying the past few days in his head. Teddy was great at computers. His mom was nowhere to be found. He always changed the subject whenever Zane brought it up. Come to think of it, which game had Teddy actually missed? Was it before the hacks began? Had he really been there for all the games in question? Zane wasn't sure anymore. What if Mr. Rempke wasn't who he seemed to be?

What if Preston was right about Teddy, and Zane had made a terrible mistake? *What if…?*

The crowd cheered again. Erik fielded a grounder and threw to Dorian to complete the 1-2-3 inning.

Zane got a sick feeling in his stomach as he jogged back to the dugout and heard the beeps fade. When they started this whole mess, the receiver was on third. Then Zane told Teddy, and the next game it had moved. Plus, Teddy didn't seem to care too much if the season ended. Was Teddy really the spy, lying to Zane, building his trust through heartfelt conversations and phony concern? All in order to use him to get information and stay one step ahead?

Zane looked at Dorian. Why did Teddy keep suggesting Dorian was the spy? To take the attention off himself, that's why. The more Zane thought about Dorian, it didn't fit. If Dorian was the spy, why would he have a Greek flag and government parking sticker on his mom's car? Wouldn't they hide that stuff?

Teddy.

Zane got back to the bench. His heart was beating fast. He sat down next to Teddy, who leaned in and whispered "Right field? Did you see it there? I saw you looking at the scoreboard."

"Yeah, I think."

"Well, if it is, I have an idea," Teddy continued. "Whenever Amber starts in right and I start on the bench, coach usually subs me in for her after three innings. Why don't you switch shoes with me. If I'm in right, I'll be able to make the download way easier than you."

CHAPTER 23

ZANE WAITED THREE seconds to speak in order to settle his nerves. It was a trick his mom used whenever she was upset with him. Now he was using it. He looked around to see if Mr. Rempke had shown up yet. He was nowhere in sight.

"Let's see how it goes," Zane said.

Zane had to fight the urge to accuse Teddy right then and there. Zane felt betrayed and used all over again. Was their friendship a total lie? He really didn't want to be right about this.

"You okay?" Teddy asked.

"Yeah. Just nervous a bit."

Zane decided to pretend like everything was normal. He put on a poker face and looked back at Teddy. Assuming Teddy was the baseball spy, at least Zane had one half of his mission completed. All Zane would have left to do was make the last download. But would he be walking into a trap set by Teddy? What was Teddy's motivation here? Either way, Zane decided he'd still get the download for Preston and explain the situation as soon as possible.

Zane was batting sixth. By the time he was up, the Renegades had already scored twice on a double by Dorian. There were two outs, and Dorian was on second. Zane took a practice swing, trying to find the grip that caused the least amount of pain.

"Be a hitter, Zane!" Rudy yelled.

The first pitch came right down the middle with no movement. It was a hitter's dream. Zane took a cut, even though he wasn't squeezing the bat fully with his left hand. When the ball struck, the bat reverberated in his hands, sending excruciating pain up his arm. The ball popped up softly to right, ending the inning. Zane did his best not to wince.

The Renegades were playing great. By the end of third, they were up 4-0, and Zane felt better about the game being won, just in case he wasn't able to make the last download. He had decided he was not going to give Teddy the shoes.

"Teddy!" Rudy shouted. "Take right. Good job out there, Amber. We'll get you back in next inning."

"Coach, can I play right and Teddy play center?" Zane asked. "Ya know, give Teddy a chance."

"I can do it," Teddy said.

"I'm sure you could, Teddy. But this is a playoff game, not practice. Zane, you have the speed, you stay in center. That's your spot. Teddy, you're a hell of a right fielder. We need you there."

The boys ran out to their spots to get the inning going. *BEEP! Beep!*

Zane knew he was close to the box, but not close enough. He tried to play it cool. The beeping continued in his ear, taunting him.

"Hey," Teddy whispered from right. "Why didn't we switch shoes?"

BEEP! Beep!

Zane put his hands up, motioning to the people all around, as if to say they were being watched and shouldn't talk.

Erik made his pitch.

The inning went by quickly. Zane, thankfully, had only one weak grounder come his way. It happened with two outs and a man on second. A batter hit one up the middle. Zane charged up toward second base to field it and was able to do the whole thing with his bare right hand. The baserunner rounded third. Zane made a perfect throw home to Sammy, who tagged the guy out easily.

"Nice play!" Sammy yelled, pointing back at Zane. They all got back to the dugout, and everybody high-fived Zane, who only offered up his healthy right hand.

By the bottom of the sixth, the Renegades led 4-2. They were one inning away from advancing.

"Teddy!" Rudy shouted. "Put it away!"

Zane looked over and saw Teddy staring at his phone.

"Coach," Teddy said, waving him over. Teddy stepped out of the dugout, and Rudy followed. Zane walked over to listen in.

"My dad got some really bad news," Teddy said. "Could I go home?"

"If you need to," Rudy said. "I'm sorry to hear that. What is it?"

"The doctor said… um." Teddy looked down. "It isn't good. I don't want to talk about it. I think I should go."

"I'm really sorry to hear that. Whatever you need to do. We'll win this sucker, and you can join us tomorrow for the semifinal if you'd like."

Teddy looked at another message coming in.

"You know what, I'm staying."

"You don't have to."

"Yes, I do. My dad's right. I want to help the team finish this last inning."

"Okay," Rudy said. "If that's what you want."

Teddy came back to the dugout. He spotted Zane. "I guess you heard all that."

"I'm really sorry. I hope you aren't staying only for me."

"For you and the team. There's too much going on here. I'll see him soon, anyways. It won't change anything. For reals."

Teddy? Acting?

Zane tried to push the words out of his head and give Teddy a sincere look of support.

Jamal lined out to end the Renegades' bottom half of the sixth inning. The game headed to the seventh.

Renegades 4, Vipers 2.

Rudy was in full-on motivation mode. "All right, Renegades! Three outs to go!"

Teddy and Zane headed to their spots in the outfield.

"Teddy, switch with me," Zane said. "Go ahead. Rudy won't notice."

"Yeah."

BEEEEEEEP!

Zane ran over to the fence in right, right next to the scoreboard. He only needed twenty seconds. Rudy was on him immediately, shouting, "I told you to stay in center, Z!"

The whole team looked at Zane. He stood there a few more seconds.

BEEEEEEEEEEEEEP!

Zane didn't move.

"Well?" Rudy asked.

CHAPTER 24

"SORRY!" ZANE SHOUTED. He lingered an extra second while everyone stared, and then left.

"Did you get it?" Teddy asked as they crossed paths on the way back to their original outfield positions. The beeping slowed down to a slower, intermittent pace.

"No swoosh. I was close."

The inning began. The entire Vipers dugout was up and yelling as loud as they could. The parents joined in, trying to will on a rally.

Teddy waited for the first pitch, then whispered something and started motioning.

Zane couldn't hear any of it over all the noise and the periodic beeping in his ear. He felt for his belt buckle and turned the volume down in his earpiece. After the next pitch, he looked back at Teddy.

"What?"

"I'll fake an injury, you run over," Teddy said.

Zane didn't respond. He didn't know what to do. Better to do this on his own, he thought. His best bet was for a hit down the right field line. Teddy would chase after it, allowing Zane to drift over from center and make the download. If not, maybe he'd just run over there after the game, saying he was still looking for his contact.

Cedric was in to pitch for Erik. The first batter grounded to Jamal at short, who threw him out easily. Cedric struck out the next batter, prompting everybody in the field to hold up two fingers. Zane realized he might not have to make the download after all. They were about to win the game. He could do it tomorrow.

"One more!" Rudy said.

"You got that, Zane?" Erik teased.

This time, nobody laughed, not even Dorian. Erik looked embarrassed. "All right, let's go!" he shouted, changing the subject.

Cedric stepped back to the mound. He was all business. He took a long look in at Sammy and rolled the ball around in his pitching hand, feeling around for the right grip. Satisfied, he twisted, raised his knee, reached back, and threw one as fast as he could—and hit the poor batter square in the back.

"Ooohhh," went the crowd.

"Sorry!" Cedric said. The kid took his base. Then, Cedric beaned the next kid as well. The next batter, a tall beanpole named Quentin, hit a single to right. The runner on second darted around the diamond and scored easily. All of a sudden, the Renegades' lead was down to 4-3, and there were runners on first and third.

Zane looked back over at Teddy, who nodded.

What did *that* mean?

Zane didn't have much time to worry. The next batter was the Vipers' cleanup man, JR Model. Model already had three hits on the day. The kid was a machine.

"You're all right, Delini!" Rudy yelled from the dugout. "One more!"

Cedric's first pitch was a perfect curveball that froze Model. Quentin, however, made a nice jump and stole second without Sammy even bothering to throw down. He was more worried about the tying run on third.

Zane tried to get Teddy's attention. "Hey," he said softly. "Teddy."

"What?"

"We're out of time. Fake the injury."

Teddy simply motioned to the mound, where Cedric was winding up. The next pitch was another curve. Model was waiting on it. He ripped one high into right-center field but playable. Zane drifted over and called off Teddy as loud as he could. "I got it!"

Teddy slowed down to give Zane room. As the ball came toward Zane, he put his bare right hand *behind* his glove—textbook, two-handed position. Then, he braced for the pain. The ball landed in his glove, but he couldn't squeeze it shut. His hand could barely move. He saw the ball pop out, almost in slow motion, and start to drop toward the grass.

Zane instinctively raised his left knee at the ball and was able to hackeysack it back up in the air, but since his knee was going up and out, the ball was now projecting away from his body. His eyes somehow located the ball, which was falling again. He whipped his right hand out and plucked the ball out of the air before he fell forward onto his right shoulder and back. He rolled back up and quickly raised the ball high to show the umpire. The ump put his fist up, signaling the out. Game over.

Renegades 4, Vipers 3.

The place went berserk. Zane's teammates sprinted out to meet him and started jumping up and down.

"Don't scare me like that!" Ricky shouted, smiling.

"All right, Zane!" Amber said.

"We're still alive," Sammy said. "Nice catch."

"Thanks, guys."

"Next time, just catch it," Amber said.

"What's the fun in that?" Zane asked.

Zane looked around and saw all his teammates enjoying the moment—all but one.

Teddy was running to the dugout. As the celebration in the outfield died down, Zane tried to focus. Something was off. He was in right center, but there were no beeps.

He heard no signal at all. He walked toward the scoreboard without making it obvious.

Nothing.

It was like the receiver had been removed from the field. He looked back at the dugout. Teddy was already gone.

CHAPTER 25

THE PLAYERS FILED off the field and gathered in front of the parking lot. Zane started digging through his bag.

Rudy started his speech. "We're not done yet!" The team cheered. "Three weeks ago you guys were close to last place. I always knew how good we could be. Now everybody knows. Tomorrow we get to play in the league semifinals. You earned it."

All the parents and players clapped again. Rudy continued. "Game's at four p.m. Get here at three fifteen p.m. You know how we're doing the pizza party after our last game? Well, the party won't be tomorrow!"

Zane went through the motions of cheering, and then finally pulled out his phone and powered it on. He stuffed the gear he had borrowed from Teddy into the borrowed bag and started to make his move out of there. He paused to fire off a message to Preston, remembering the instructions to not say anything of value over a text.

I figured it out, he texted. *Spy and receiver are on the move. Call me!*

He slipped the phone into his back pocket of his baseball pants and started walking fast.

"Hey, wait up," Amber said.

"Oh, hey. Sorry, but I really gotta go."

"What's the matter? Is it Teddy's dad? Are you going over there?"

"No, I have to get home. Sorry." Zane turned from her once again.

"I'm walking this way, too. I'll join you."

Zane looked at his phone. No response yet. He started to say something to Amber, but she cut him off.

"My dad couldn't come pick me up." Amber flashed her killer smile. "I really don't want to walk alone. So, thanks for walking with me, even if it's just for a few minutes."

"I don't have a few minutes," Zane said. "I'm really sorry." He started walking.

"Zane, you're being rude."

"I'll explain later, sorry!" he shouted without turning back. He picked up his pace. He took out his phone and called Preston. As it rang, Zane considered his options. He could go home and wait for him, but that didn't seem too smart since Teddy was getting away. He imagined sprinting to Teddy's house, knocking on the door and demanding the receiver. How would that play out? The call went to voicemail again.

After he walked a block, he got to the corner store where he needed to turn left. He looked back and saw Amber still following him. Zane checked his phone and saw nothing. He texted again.

Where are you? Call ASAP. Emergency!

He sighed, realizing he needed to standby to see what Preston wanted to do. Amber was picking up her pace. He decided to wait for her, since he had to wait for instructions, anyways.

Amber hustled up to him.

"I wasn't trying to ditch you," Zane said.

"Well, you did," she snapped back. "What's going on? Why are you acting like this? You've been weird all day."

"Just stressed out. You know. I don't really want to talk about it. Sorry."

"Fine. Which intersection do you live near?"

"Crocker and Fifth."

"Oh, I'm right on Buchanan," she said. "It's way quicker to cut through the alley this way. I do it all the time. C'mon."

Zane thought about how badly he wanted to get Amber out of his way. "Okay, sure."

They headed to the side of the building and entered the alley.

"What kind of hearing aid is that?" she asked.

Startled, Zane reached for his hair to see if it was covering his ear. "What hearing aid?"

"The one you're touching. The one you started wearing last week."

"Oh, yeah. You got me. I hate this stupid thing. It's embarrassing."

"Who cares? Nobody would care."

Zane heard the car coming before he saw it. The black sedan screeched to a halt at the end of the alley, blocking Amber and Zane's path. The door opened. Shorty jumped out and put up his hands. The gun was in a holster on his belt, this time in plain sight.

"Hold it right there," Shorty said cooly.

"Amber, run!" Zane screamed. As he turned to retreat, Amber grabbed his arm with a force he did not know she possessed. Her killer smile was gone.

He looked back at her, astonished, and tried to yank free. Shorty stepped closer.

"What are you doing?" Zane yelled at Amber. "We have to go!"

She came at him with her other arm and snapped something hard and metal tight around his left wrist.

Handcuffs.

"Zane Mitchell," she said. "We're United States Federal Agents. We need to talk."

CHAPTER 26

"AMBER!" SHORTY SNAPPED. "I said I needed to handle this part. This is where you stay away. How many times did we go over this?"

Zane panicked. "What's he talking about? Lemme go!"

The other end of the handcuff was attached to Amber's wrist. Shorty kept walking up. Ignoring the pain in his left hand, Zane yanked his handcuffed wrist backward as hard as he could, pulling Amber's body toward him and knocking her off balance. They both started to fall. In a flash, Amber dug her shoulder into Zane's stomach, and drove him to the ground. He landed hard on his butt, nearly on top of an old bike rack. Amber was bent forward and crouched low but still on her feet. She immediately circled around behind him and put him in a headlock. Zane's arm was bent backward. She was in complete control. She looked up at Shorty and said, "I got this, see?"

Shorty shook his head. "That's beside the point."

"My shoulder," Zane said. "You're ripping it apart."

Amber was as calm as could be. "Sorry, Zane, but you've got to chill."

Zane tried to scream but had no air. Amber relaxed her grip but only a little.

"I'm not here to hurt you kid," Shorty said, holding up his ID for inspection. "I never was. I'm Special Agent Rex Wilson. I, unlike my daughter here, work for something called the CRU."

Amber let go.

"Your dau...?" Zane couldn't get the thought out. He felt a few quick movements, followed by a clinking sound. Zane pulled his arm and realized he was now handcuffed to the bicycle rack. She came around to his front and looked back at Wilson, who was still upset at her.

"It's true," she told Zane. "And we'd love to know what you've been doing."

"Amber—" Wilson began.

"Dad, we're not in danger. Let me stay and talk to him."

"You don't know that," he said.

"We have a connection," she said. "He'll talk to me. You need me here to help figure this out."

Wilson sighed, signaling he had lost another argument with his feisty teenager.

Zane felt like he was in a dream where nothing made sense. *They* were CRU? Did they know his mom? He had no idea who to trust, so he stayed quiet. Wilson stepped forward. "Here." He showed Zane the earpiece he had lost. "We saw you drop this last week. I see you got a new one."

"What do you need a hidden wireless audio relay system for?" Amber asked. "And why have you been snooping around our equipment the past few games?"

Zane thought about playing dumb, but they were holding the earpiece and looking right at him. His shoulder and his hand ached. The air in his lungs finally returned. "How do I know I can trust you?"

Wilson snorted. "You want to know how you can trust us? That's funny, coming from a kid who was caught red-handed attempting to steal government files. You're the one who's in question here. You're the one who's been messing with my operation. You just triggered *another* alarm."

The badge looked very real. None of this made sense. "You're not a Federal Agent," Zane said. "That ID is fake."

"We are," Amber said.

"You're fourteen years old!"

"Okay, I'm not an agent yet, but I will be. And I don't know what you think is going on here, but you need to start talking. We need to know who put you up to this, where you're taking those files, and why."

Zane could see into Wilson's car. It was unmarked on the outside but had a dashboard full of computers and screens. Zane's phone finally rang. He ignored it.

"That's why I'm doing this," Zane said. "Your co-worker. Or so you say."

"What?" Wilson and Amber said simultaneously.

The ringing continued. Zane silenced it.

"I'm doing this whole thing for the Cybersecurity Reinforcement Unit," Zane said. "That's why I don't believe you. I have a mission to do, and you had no idea. If you *really* were CRU, you would've known about it. I don't know if I can trust you."

"First off, this whole setup is ours," Amber said. *"You* are the one crashing the party, messing with our stuff."

"My stuff," Wilson corrected.

Amber kept looking at Zane while she spoke. "Looking for your 'lost contact' that you don't really wear. Or your 'hearing aid' you suddenly needed."

Zane sat there silently as Amber continued. "Secondly, we've shown you my dad's badge. And explained the tech. There's more gear in the car. The computer. Is that all fake, too? We told you how we caught you."

"Amber, that's quite enough," Wilson said sternly. "Zane, you seem like a nice young man. I could arrest you if you want and make it official. Or we can talk. You know we're telling the truth. That's why you didn't answer your phone. Now let's straighten this out. Who's calling? Who at the CRU put you up to this?"

"Preston Burnett."

Amber looked at Wilson, who shook his head.

"I don't know him," Wilson said. "Describe him."

"Older, white guy. Early sixties maybe. Tall, seems to be in pretty good shape. Going bald kinda. Worries a lot."

"That doesn't exactly narrow it down," Wilson said. "What happened?"

"He showed up at my house last Saturday and said he needed my help. He told me about the Link, and how there was a weak spot at Falcon Field. He said one of my teammates was a spy, secretly downloading the OIL files onto the receiver. He didn't want me to stop it from happening, he just wanted me to copy whatever was on the receiver and take it to him. I was about to tell him how Teddy was the spy, but I guess I was wrong."

Amber looked at her dad. "Flanagan behind this?"

"Maybe, but why send a kid?" Wilson said. "Hold on." He took out his cell phone and made a call. They sat in silence while it rang, each unanswered ring aggravating Wilson even more. "Tyndall, it's Rex. Call me!" Wilson hung up, then fired off a text.

"Okay, where were we?" Wilson asked.

"What's happening?" Zane asked.

"You're being used by somebody," Wilson said.

"Huh?"

"I believe you, Zane," Wilson said. "I'll explain first so we can figure this out. I'm a former lead field agent that recently joined the CRU. I was the one that had this theory that if you set up the right equipment in the exact right spot, a hacker might be able to enter into the Link and download files. Theoretically. These files could do some deadly damage to our country."

"Right, that's what Preston said."

"So, how do you test a weakness in your defense?" Wilson asked.

Amber jumped in with the answer. "You try to break in to see how a criminal would do it."

"You've been breaking into your own system, just to see how it's done?" Zane asked.

"That's how you shore up your defenses," Wilson said. "That's what we've been doing. Cybersecurity, reinforced."

Wilson nodded. His phone rang. He didn't answer right away. "I'm pretty hot right now. You two stay in the car. I'll talk outside. Amber, you fill him in on the *real* mission." He got up and slammed the car door as he shouted into the phone.

CHAPTER 27

"BACK IN LATE May, I read my dad's e-mail when he fell asleep," Amber said.

"What does this have to do with it?" Zane asked.

"Everything," she said. "That's why we're here. That, and my dad's bosses are egomaniacs. Anyways, I've always tried to learn about my dad's missions and stuff, but he obviously never let me. It was waaay off limits. I got lucky two months ago when he fell asleep while looking at his phone. I figured I'd take a peek before the screen locked. I couldn't resist."

"That doesn't surprise me," Zane said.

Amber took it as a compliment. "I read this massive chain. I couldn't stop. I learned the CRU has big computer servers that needed these crucial upgrades. The process was going to take two weeks, and they had to do it in late July. Had to. But my dad studied it and had a theory that while the servers were being upgraded, that process might create a weak spot in the Link's defense. He told them not to do the upgrade yet because it might leave our government secrets temporarily unprotected from the weak spot. Why take that chance without first checking out his theory? That's the whole point of the CRU. But they said there was a zero percent chance he was right. This boss guy Flanagan showed him all these charts as proof. They said it would be more dangerous to not get the server upgrades ASAP. Then Flanagan was being such a jerk to my dad, bringing up all these times my dad was wrong about stuff since he joined the unit. And how he wasn't as smart as the guys that designed the Link. Flanagan said my dad's test might mess up the upgrades. My dad shot back. I couldn't believe the tone he took with his boss. I was sure he'd get fired. They each think the other is trying to make them look bad. They act like ninth graders. Flanagan said he would even watch Falcon Field on surveillance cameras to make sure my dad didn't disobey. It made me so mad to read it. The egos over there are crazy. After I read all this, I was so upset. I woke my dad up and asked him about it. I had to."

"Was he pissed at you?" Zane asked.

"That's one way to put it," she said. "But since I'd read so much already and was worried, he said he would calm me down. He said his immediate boss, Borchers, actually agreed with him. Borchers said the server upgrades had to happen but encouraged my dad to go to Falcon Field during those two weeks and test out his weak spot theory, as long as this Flanagan idiot didn't find out and start an interoffice war. So, my dad needed to go onto the field and operate the receiver once a day during this time but was nervous about doing so. Flanagan really was crazy enough to watch the field. He could tap into any number of cameras to do it. My dad didn't want to get fired."

"So, you raised your hand," Zane said.

"Bingo. You see, that stuff I told you about softball really was the truth. So, when I read all these e-mails, I realized I could kill two birds with one stone—play sports and help my dad. I convinced him that if I signed up for the league, I'd be able to help him run the tests while I blended in with the team. I could do his job for him during the games, and nobody would know. I also convinced him there was no danger, just me pushing a few buttons for him during a game. It was the perfect solution. My objective was to discreetly hide the receiver between the foul lines where it would work, monitor it, and see if I could download the OIL files during the games. My dad disguised himself as Shorty and hung around to keep an eye on things."

"So, what happened?" Zane asked.

"Two things," Amber said. "First, the big one. His theory was right. We figured out how to hack into the Link. It took a few days, but we finally got the first OIL file we needed in order to prove that Dad was right. So, Dad fessed up to his boss, who should have kissed his feet and apologized, but instead, he just told Dad to continue his testing mission to fully understand how hacking from the weak spot worked. Then, we had an even bigger problem."

Just then, Wilson came back in the car. "They're still checking on Preston Burnett. Where are you in the story?"

"We found out we were right about the weak spot," Amber said.

"I'm still waiting for that apology," Wilson said. "I was

right. And I was very nice about it when I filed my formal mission report. Mostly nice."

"What happened next?" Zane asked.

"Somebody started interfering," she said. "The tampering sensor my dad invented went off Monday during the makeup game. We couldn't figure out why somebody would mess with the receiver during the game. Since the server upgrades couldn't be stopped, we had to keep going with our testing mission. But we really wanted to know who was messing with us."

"Dorian was on my radar first," Wilson said. "We also tracked that awful Erik kid, and a few more. Then you started acting all funny."

Wilson tossed Zane his old bat bag that he had stolen a few days earlier. It landed next to him in the backseat. "Sorry about taking this," Wilson said. "I thought I could check out your stuff without blowing my cover. I had to."

"Sorry about punching you in the nuts," Zane said, even though he wasn't.

Wilson waved his hand. "Is there anything else you can tell me about Preston?"

"He seems pretty high-ranking," Zane said. "Knows his stuff. Dresses nice. Wears those stupid bow ties."

Wilson's body jerked forward. "Bow ties?"

"Yeah, what?"

Wilson pounded away at his keyboard. "I think I…. Hold on. Here! Is this your Preston?"

Zane looked at the screen. "Yeah. That's Preston Burnett. You know him?"

"I do," Wilson said. "But that man's real name is Parker Boone."

"Parker Boone? He kept the same initials. That's not very good spycraft. Why'd he give me a fake name and do all this? Is he one of Flanagan's guys?"

"I wish it *were* that. This guy isn't with the government anymore. Parker Boone's bad news. Why would he... wait. He...."

Wilson squinted his eyes shut. He started mumbling to himself, almost like he was praying.

"Dad?" Amber asked.

Wilson held up his hand. Then, he opened his eyes wide, and his jaw dropped.

"What!" Zane and Amber both shouted.

"I got it!" Wilson said. "It all fits. Hold on." Wilson whipped out his walkie-talkie and pushed a button.

"Go ahead," said the voice.

"You're never going to believe this. It's Boone. He's back. He tricked some kid on the team into helping him get the OIL files. Put out an APB. I'm almost done talking to the kid. Mitchell. Zane Mitchell. I'll get back to you ASAP. Over."

Zane was completely lost. He looked over at Amber, who also looked a bit confused.

"Okay, from the top. The man you know as Preston Burnett is actually Parker Boone," Wilson said again. "He's a traitor. He's former CRU. Three years ago he was accused of selling secrets overseas to our enemies. It was a legal mess. The charges were eventually dropped due to problems with the evidence, but he's guilty as sin, and we all knew it. We followed him around for a year, but he sued the government for unjustly harassing him, so ultimately we backed off a bit. Since then, he's done his best to stay off the grid. But he's plugged in somehow, or with someone."

"What do you mean?" Amber asked.

Zane looked back and forth.

"Think about it," Wilson said. "It all adds up. Parker must have somehow seen that mission report I filed, but it didn't have Amber's name in it, thankfully. All Parker saw was a golden chance falling into his lap... a detailed plan that resulted in the OIL files sitting out on Falcon Field, ripe for the picking. It was his chance to get the OIL and finish what he started three years ago. But he can't go stand in the middle of Falcon Field himself because I would have spotted him. Or the cameras would have. And he didn't know which kid had been helping me. He needed that kid, Amber, to keep showing up and downloading the OIL files onto that receiver so he could get what he wanted. So, how does he physically get himself to the receiver without being seen? On his own, he's stuck. He needed help."

"He needed me," Zane said.

"Yup," Wilson said. "He recruits you by pretending he's the head of the CRU and making up a bogus story about a bad guy downloading files. He tricks you into making copies and bringing them to him. To 'help' the CRU. Zane, tell me I'm right. Start chiming in here."

"That's exactly it," Zane said.

"Pretty brilliant," Amber said. "So, I hack in and download the OIL files onto the receiver, then Parker and Zane come along and copy the good stuff right from underneath our noses, without us knowing it."

"Oh, crap," Zane said.

"What?" Wilson asked.

"So, I gave him the list of codenames and agents?" Zane asked.

"He got the list of codenames, which can be changed," Wilson said. "Thankfully, once we suspected tampering, Amber began downloading fake OIL files, just to be safe. That way we could continue the testing mission. The second file—the list of names you gave him—was fake. But he doesn't know that, and he's still after the decoder key, which he'll never get."

"What you are telling me makes way more sense than what Preston said," Zane said.

"You mean Parker," Wilson said.

"Yeah, Parker," Zane said. "His story never fully added up. I kept asking him why he didn't just go in there himself and get the box immediately. He said the spy had surveillance, and he didn't want the spy to know we were on to him."

"In reality," Amber said, "he wanted me to keep downloading files from the Link, and you to keep copying what I got. You were his accomplice, and you didn't even know it."

Zane thought back to all he had done for that man and all the damage he'd caused. "I feel sick."

"Don't," Amber said.

"Parker said I needed to find the baseball spy and get those files to help save my country. Well, I finally found the spy. It was… it was me."

"You had no idea," Amber said. "You thought you were doing the right thing."

"He was with me in my house," Zane said, shaking at

the thought. "Not anymore, thankfully. But what if he hid some cameras or something?"

"We can check for those," Wilson said.

"Parker wanted to know which of the players was operating the receiver," Amber said. "Who knows what his plans are once he finds out."

"So, Teddy's not a spy?" Zane asked.

"Why Teddy?" she asked.

"After the game, he ran off fast, like he had taken it. Like the whole thing with his dad was just a lie to get out of there."

"Our receiver is still there," Wilson said. "I'm looking at it right now through the video feed on my laptop. Are you sure your earpiece was working?"

"My belt! Oh my gosh, I forgot. I lowered the volume so I could hear Teddy talk. He didn't take the receiver after all. If my volume was up, I would have heard it sitting right there by the fence. Teddy was running off to be with his dad. I feel horrible."

"Teddy Rempke is no spy," Amber said. "He's Teddy. And his dad does have cancer. His mom hasn't been in the picture for a long time. We checked him out when we were trying to figure out who was interfering with our mission. You had no way of knowing. Parker was messing with your head."

"Dorian was my other guess," Zane said.

"Crazy story with that guy, but not a spy. I'll tell you more later."

Zane's phone rang again.

Wilson's hand shot out like a cobra and grabbed it. "You're not answering yet. We have to game plan here. I want to go back to something. This fake mission Parker gave you. You weren't actually stopping the 'spy.' Didn't that seem weird to you? That there was no end in sight. And what about your parents during all this?"

"My dad passed three years ago. But to answer your question, Parker kept saying we had some more time to work with. We could help the bigger picture by finding out who the spy was working for. I kept arguing the point, saying it was my mom's life on the line." Zane had been so busy piecing this together he hadn't considered what it all meant for his mom.

"Your mom?" Amber asked. "What does this have to do—"

"You didn't know?" Zane blurted out. "She's an undercover operative. My dad was, too. They're on the OIL. I saw their codenames on the first file I copied."

"What?" Amber said. "Dad, did you know that?"

"No way," Wilson said. "If they're undercover, we wouldn't have known. We probably have never even seen her."

"It's true," Zane said. "Our lives would've been ruined if all those lists got out in the open. We have to let her know what's going on. Can you call her at Langley? She's somewhere there but not allowed to have her cell phone."

Wilson leaned forward and wiped his forehead. He spoke slowly. "That doesn't sound right. Why do you think she's at CRU Headquarters right now?"

"Because Parker said that's what happens during a crisis. She's stuck there until this is solved. Nobody in the CRU is allowed to make personal calls because it's such a sensitive operation. I haven't been able to call her at all."

"When did you talk to her last?" Wilson asked.

"Saturday. Right when this all started. Parker came inside my house and he called her at work. I talked to her. My mom even gave Parker her keys."

"Are you sure it was your mom on the phone?"

Zane looked at Amber for reassurance but got none. "Her voice was distorted from security filters, so she stayed quiet most of the conversation. But it was her."

"That wasn't your mom," Wilson said gravely.

"Yes it was! My mom even said she tried to call my old babysitter."

"Did you say the babysitter's name first, or did she?"

Zane thought back to the conversation. "I did. But it was her, I could tell."

"No. It was a trick, along with everything else that man has told you."

Zane swallowed hard, almost too afraid to ask. "What are you saying?"

Wilson raised his walkie-talkie again. His body was tense. "I need Tyndall, ASAP." Wilson told Zane, "Tyndall deals with OIL. He'll know. What's her name?"

"Mallory Clayborn."

"Clayborn?" Wilson asked.

"Yes," Zane answered.

"Hello, again," the voice said.

"Ben, quick. I need to know right now if an undercover CRU agent Mallory Clayborn is in-house at this exact moment, doing some overnight legwork or crisis management that would take a few days or longer."

"Nobody has anything like that going on right now," the voice said. *"And, hold on… it says here she hasn't even en-*

*tered the building in over a week. She was due for time off
after completing her last mission. She isn't even expected back
at CRU for another ten days."*

Amber put her hand over her mouth.

"Wilson, what does that mean?" Zane whispered,
turning white.

"Tyndall," Wilson said. "We have an agent in trouble.
Mallory Clayborn is missing and in extreme danger. Parker Boone is involved somehow."

"Boone?" Tyndall asked. *"We just put out the APB. Our
agents are heading out. They're going to arrest him as soon as
they see him."*

"Cancel that order!" Wilson shouted into the phone.
"Cancel it *NOW!*"

CHAPTER 28

"AGENT CLAYBORN WILL be killed the moment we move in on Parker Boone!" Wilson pleaded into the walkie-talkie.

"Oh, no—he's right," Amber said.

"Okay, okay," Tyndall said. *"Just hold on. I'm telling them now."*

Zane, Wilson and Amber heard Tyndall speak into his radio. *"Agents, stand down. I repeat. Stand down and await further instructions. Do not pursue the suspect."*

Then, Tyndall came back to his walkie talkie. *"Okay Wilson, I'm trusting you. I need an explanation."*

"So do I," Zane said. "Where's my mom?"

"Parker abducted her," Wilson said. "He needed her out of the picture in order to use you. Maybe he used her to get more information, I don't know. I don't think he wants to kill her unless he has to. Right now, in his mind, he doesn't have to. Not yet at least. He doesn't have the decoder key for the OIL. He'll come to the game tomorrow, hoping you finally get it. He may want Amber, too, once he finds out it's her. If he thinks something has changed and we are on to him, then he'll end the game he's playing and eliminate your mom."

"He won't be able to kill anybody if we arrest him," Zane said.

"But his partner could," Amber said, putting it all together. "He's not acting alone. That's why we're in a tough spot here."

"You mean the voice on the phone, pretending to be my mom?" Zane asked.

"Exactly," Wilson said. "That had to be his partner. Parker would have needed help abducting your mom, getting those car keys, and fooling you. The partner is probably holding your mom hostage right now. From his point of view, if Parker gets arrested or killed, there's no reason to keep your mom alive anymore. She's a witness. We need to find out where your mom is before we make a move on either one of these guys. Bottom line, it's the best chance we have at ensuring her survival."

"How are we going to do that?" Zane asked.

The phone chimed with another text from Parker.

Answer. If you are not in a position to talk, text me now. What is your status? Receiver? Spy? Update ASAP.

Wilson and Amber looked at Zane.

"What?" Zane asked.

"There's a way, but you would need to meet him," Wilson said.

"Is that safe?" Zane asked.

"I don't like it, but it may be necessary," Wilson said. "As long as Parker thinks he has you fooled, and you are helping him, he has no reason to hurt you. He needs you. So, if you play it cool and do what we need, we can figure out where your mom is. If you suddenly run away or don't head home to meet him, he's going to know something's up. That could be the end for her."

Zane was thinking it over.

Wilson continued. "We can have agents hiding right outside your house and also watching and listening through cameras and windows. All that being said, you would be taking a risk. I can't make you do this. But if you do, I will do everything I can to keep you protected."

Zane held up his phone, showing the unanswered text. "What's the plan?"

CHAPTER 29

ZANE'S FINGERS SHOOK as he worked his phone.

Parker, posing as Preston, answered before the first ring even finished. *"Where are you? Where's the receiver?"*

"Sorry, I couldn't talk," Zane said. "Walking home still. I had a bunch of kids around me and couldn't break away. But the most important thing is that I was wrong. The receiver is not on the move. It's still at Falcon Field."

"That's okay as long as you got the download. Tell me you got it."

"I think."

"Quit messing around. Did you get it or not?"

"My earpiece stopped working halfway through the game. I didn't realize it at the time, but my volume was turned down. It was a bad mistake, I know. But I went right up to the spot where I heard it before and waited twenty seconds."

"Okay, that sounds promising," Parker said. *"I'll check it in a second. And the spy?"*

"Amber Hyatt," Zane said. "I saw her messing with the receiver. It's her. One hundred percent."

"Huh. Interesting. Wasn't my guess. Excellent work. I'll be at your house in two minutes. Can you get there quickly?"

Moments later, Zane arrived home. Parker Boone was waiting for him, just like the first day they met. Only this time, it was Zane tricking Parker.

Zane led him inside, and they both sat down at the kitchen table. Once they were inside, Wilson and Amber drove up Crocker Street and parked four houses down, listening to the audio being delivered from the tiny microphone they had taped inside Zane's shirt. Wilson had told Zane two other agents were hiding somewhere outside his house, listening in and ready to bust in at a moment's notice.

"How's my mom doing?" Zane asked. "Have you talked to her?"

"Oh," Parker said. "Yes, she's working hard. Just asked about you. Hopefully this is the end of everything right here."

Zane clenched his fist under the table. He wondered where Parker had been the past few days.

"So, let's have it," Parker said.

Zane got out his right cleat, popped out the card, and handed it to Parker.

"Thanks," Parker said. He slid the card into his laptop, drumming his fingers on the table while it loaded. Zane sat silently.

Parker grunted. "You didn't get anything. You didn't make a download."

"I was sure I was over there long enough."

Parker backed away from the table and walked around the room, fidgeting with his bowtie. He stopped to look at himself in the hallway mirror. He took a deep breath and sat back down across from Zane.

"It's okay," he said with a nervous smile. "It's going to be okay."

The hair on Zane's neck stood up as he imagined what was going on inside Parker's head and how that impacted his and his mom's survival. "What now?" Zane managed to say.

Parker sat in thought.

Zane waited, figuring the less he spoke, the less chance he had of messing up.

Finally, Parker popped out the micro SD card and handed it back to Zane. "We're out of time," Parker said. "You're correct. We need to pull the plug on this whole thing. Tomorrow. One way or another, we need to end this tomorrow."

"What do you mean?"

"We'll pick up Amber after the semifinal game," Parker said. "That's the best place to get her. And you're getting that download tomorrow, no matter what."

"You're going to the game again?" Zane asked.

"You won't see me there, but I'll be there. The main thing is for you to make the download. I don't care if you fake a seizure in right field to buy yourself time, you do it. I don't care if Amber suspects something. By then it won't matter. I will come get your cleats from you as soon as the time is right. I'll be watching."

"Where are you going to be exactly?"

"I'd rather not say," Parker said. "Better that way."

"And what about Amber? What are you going to do?"

"Don't worry about that traitor," Parker said. "We'll take her in as soon as the game is over. Your family's identity will be safe. You'll be done, and your mom will finally get to come home. This will all be over tomorrow."

Zane forced a smile. Parker got up to leave.

"Thanks for everything, Zane," he said. "You've been a great help to your country."

"Sorry I didn't get the job done faster."

"You did great." The disgraced former agent walked out the front door and closed it behind him.

Zane exhaled. "I sure did," he said, holding up the micro SD card that had just infected Parker's computer.

CHAPTER 30

ZANE WATCHED OUT the window as Parker drove down the street and turned the corner. A moment later, Wilson's car pulled up from the other direction. Amber jumped out, and two agents—an older man and a woman—appeared out of nowhere and got in the backseat. Once they were in, Wilson sped off to follow Parker. Zane opened the front door, and Amber came bounding in.

"You crushed it," Amber said. "Get the phone, hurry."

Zane went over to his duffel bag and took out the government cell phone Amber had slipped in there earlier. It was on silent but showed an incoming call.

"Hello?"

"Zane, that was excellent," Wilson said. *"When he put that SD card in his laptop, he screwed himself. It's called a 'mirror relay.' Now every time he opens that laptop, we can see what his screen sees. It's just what we needed. Plus, it has a GPS tracker. We're in business. I'm with Agents Reyes and McNally. We have him on our screen now."*

"Great. Do you think he's headed to my mom?"

"Hard to say," Wilson said. *"But we are definitely ready for that scenario. The CRU also has a fully geared-up Tactical Rescue Team mobilized and looped into our GPS feed and radio. They know to stay close by in case this turns into a hostage situation. They also know not to be seen unless we call them in."*

"Let's say he isn't headed to see my mom. Then what?"

"Then nothing has changed, right?" Amber said. "We still can't take him in."

"Correct," Wilson said. *"We need to keep waiting and track his communications."*

Zane's silence on the phone conveyed his dissatisfaction with the situation.

Wilson pressed on. *"The mirror relay you planted is a game-changer for us. Parker will be routing his calls and messages through his laptop's security program. So, whether he's texting or calling from his phone, or using messages from his computer, we've got him. I know you want us to make a move on him now, but that would be too risky. We've simply got to have more information. Hang on, he's turning."*

"Where are you?" Zane asked.

"I'll stay on the line with you," Wilson said. *"We're east. Here we go. He's pulling into a motel... yup, he's heading in. We'll be parking across the street to observe."*

Zane could hear Wilson speaking into a radio. *"Rescue Team, this is Wilson. Suspect is turning into the Capital City Motel. He's parking at the far west end, in front of the last room on the end. I can't make out the room number yet. Situation is still surveil only. What's your twenty?"*

The radio hissed, and then a voice came on. *"Affir-*

mative. We've got your signal. We're a block behind you on Fourteenth, can be there in seconds."

"Copy, stand by," Wilson said.

"Is my mom there?" Zane asked hurriedly.

"That's what we're here to find out," Wilson said. *"But Parker is still sitting in his car. We can't move into position yet. We have to wait. If we move now, he might catch us when he's getting out of his car and walking to his room. As soon as he's inside, we'll get a bit closer and set things up. I have all my toys ready."*

"'Kay," Zane said.

"I'll tell you as soon as I see something," Wilson said. *"But he's just sitting there."*

Zane waited for a few more seconds before speaking up. "Any movement? Anything from the mirror relay?"

"Not since five seconds ago," Wilson said, annoyed. *"I promise we'll tell you when he gets out."*

"Sorry," Zane said. "This is torture. I just can't sit here and wait any longer."

"Well, you have to," Wilson said. *"Welcome to the world of stakeouts. Amber, talk to him about something else."*

"Dorian is government," she said. "Greek."

"What?"

"You were right about him," she said. "We knew about his family, so naturally I suspected he was the one messing with the receiver."

"But he wasn't," Zane said.

"Correct. Dorian's a normal kid. Sorta. He and his mom moved here three months ago. He carries around a lot of anger because of what happened back home."

"What happened?"

"His mom is the ambassador for the Greek Embassy in D.C. That explains his English skills. His dad's Italian originally, but he stayed back in Greece. You're right about Dorian lying. I heard him tell the guys he was from New York. He wants nothing to do with his Greek heritage right now. If your mom was a Greek politician, you'd probably lie about it, too."

"Why? And what's happening at the motel?"

Wilson spoke up. *"Nothing. He's still in the car, and we're still watching. Anyways, here's the short version. There was a huge economic collapse in Greece. There were riots, violent protests, all of it. Politicians became targets. Dorian told Amber that all of his friends turned on him. His family was pretty much chased out of there. His mom was lucky because she has a good job in the U.S. But the kid's shell-shocked."*

"That doesn't give him the right to be such a jackwagon," Zane said.

"I think it's his defense mechanism," Amber said. "He wanted to let people know not to mess with him. But he's gotten better, he really has. I know how he comes across, but a lot of it's misunderstood. When he asked me out, that was the first time he ever came out of his shell."

"That's why he was so mad at Teddy," Zane said.

"Yeah, that was a big deal for him," Amber said.

"All right, story time's over," Wilson said as he raised his binoculars. *"He's headed to the room. This is odd, but his face looks pretty red, almost like he's been...."*

"What?" Zane asked.

"Crying, I think." Wilson picked up the radio. *"Rescue, he's inside the motel room. We're moving into the parking lot. Maintain your distance."*

"Copy."

Wilson drove across the street and entered the parking lot. He parked next to a few other cars but distanced himself from Parker's room. The agent took out a laptop-sized radio transmitter and set it on the console.

Zane spoke up again into the phone. "Can you see—"

Amber held up a hand to shush him. "Let him work."

Zane ignored her. "How will you be able to tell if she's in there?"

"We can see through walls," Wilson said. *"It's a transmitter called RF-Pose. It beams out radio waves that pass through walls. The waves that hit human bodies are reflected back because of our bodies' high water content. AI translates the data into stick figures and puts it on the screen in real time. MIT developed it."*

Zane followed along, then heard Wilson speak into the radio. *"Bad news Rescue, only one stick figure on the screen. I scanned the whole room, and Agent Clayborn is not here. Back off another block. Unless the situation changes, this will not be a rescue. I don't want you to be seen, but I don't want to cut you loose just yet."*

"At least we still get to see what he's up to," Amber said. "As in right now. Look."

Zane and Amber saw the screen flash and become very bright.

"Dad, it's showing up on the phone. Is this what I think it is?"

"Yes," Wilson said. *"He's on his laptop. I've routed the screen to your phone."*

Zane realized he was looking at Parker's computer screen. The background image was Parker Boone, probably ten years' younger, posing with a younger man that looked just like Parker. They were on a mountain range somewhere on a sunny day, smiling big. The younger man, mid-twenties in the picture, was holding a dog with his muscular right arm. His left arm was draped over Parker's shoulder. It was a beautiful image.

Parker's mouse began moving around the screen. Zane felt a thrill as he watched Parker's movements. Parker clicked on a messaging icon, and a box opened up.

"Are you guys getting this?" Zane asked.

"Oh, yeah," Wilson said. *"Jackpot. We can continue talking while your screen is mirroring Parker's. He can't hear us. Looks like the show is about to start."*

Parker typed in a series of passwords that appeared as black circles. Finally, the messaging began.

PB: ?
SHARK: GO.
PB: Z EMPTY. MISSING KEY.
SHARK: BAD PLAN. ABORT.
PB: FINAL SHOT. TOMORROW. SPIDER ID'D - GIRL. CATCH FLIES. NAB SPIDER.
SHARK: NO KEY NO EXTRACTION.
PB: GOOSE SECURE?
SHARK: PEN OPEN AFTER KEY, SPIDER SE-CURE.

The exchange stalled. After ten seconds, Zane couldn't hold in his question any longer. "Goose?"

"Your mom, probably," Wilson said. *"Mother Goose. Wait, there's more.*

SHARK: BE AT WEB. KEEP POSTED.
PB: OVER.

Zane's screen went black. "What happened?" he said into the phone.

"He shut his laptop," Wilson said.

"What were they saying? Did you understand it?"

"Here's what I think. We know his partner is this Shark guy. Parker convinced him to come tomorrow. Great news."

"I'm Spider?" Amber asked.

Wilson frowned. *"Yeah. They want you, but we will have so many people on you so fast the second they try anything."*

"Dad, it's okay," she said.

Wilson paused for a moment. *"Anyway, we were spot on with our theory and our strategy. He and his partner are holding Mallory. She's alive, Zane. Mother Goose."*

"What do you think?" Zane asked. "Will they let her go? She's in the pen? It's gonna open?"

"That's the best-case scenario," Wilson said. *"Parker and Shark will both be there tomorrow to get the key from you, possibly get Amber, make an escape—their extraction—then release Mallory somehow."*

"But what reason do they have to release her after they get what they want?" Zane asked. "Especially if they try for Amber?"

"All we know is their plan will never make it that far. We'll arrest them together by the first inning and figure out where your mom is."

"Do I have to show up at the game?" Zane asked. "You guys can just swoop in and grab Shark and Parker."

"We don't even know who Shark is or where Parker will be," Amber said. "We have to go in there like it was any other game."

"Agreed," Wilson said. *"You need to be there. Don't do anything to scare Shark and Parker away. That would be the worst-case scenario for Mallory—and for the both of you. This is the safest thing to do. We have people that will look into everything we've got on this 'Shark.' Starting this second, we're looking for him and your mom. It's only a matter of time."*

"Got it," Zane said. "Amber, but what about you? Are you okay? This is real."

"I can handle myself. I'm more worried about you."

"Why?" he asked.

"We need to get you ready," she said. "Tomorrow's a big day."

CHAPTER 31

FRIDAY'S SEMIFINAL GAME had finally come. Zane still had the earpiece, belt buckle, and cleats Parker had given him, but he was wearing them strictly for show. He wanted Parker to think he intended to use them.

The earpiece, however, was now being used to communicate with the CRU. Wilson had altered it so he and the other agents could speak directly to Zane. Zane had a microphone the size of a pencil eraser sewn into the neckline of his jersey. He was walking alone to Falcon Field, although he knew the CRU was watching him.

"Zane, if you can hear me, cough twice," Wilson said.

He did as he was asked.

"We see you and copy you loud and clear. Be advised. We may have a breakthrough on intel with Shark. We may have his image and even audio of another conversation that happened late last night between him and Parker."

Zane had another mile to walk but was pretty paranoid that Shark was also watching him.

He didn't risk saying anything into his mic, though.

Thankfully, Wilson continued filling him in. *"Our surveillance team saw a food delivery man drop an order off at Parker's motel room last night at nine. We didn't think much of it at the time. There were other food deliveries made last night to motel guests as well. We figured Parker was just eating dinner. But when the morning agent checked the video we got, her fresh set of eyes told her Parker's expression seemed a bit off during the delivery. We didn't have much else though. The delivery guy had a jacket showing he was from the Ming Dragon Star restaurant. And guess what? Actually, don't guess because we don't want you to talk right now, but there is no Ming Dragon Star restaurant. We think it was Shark! On one hand, we're annoyed we could have had him. On the other hand, this helps a ton. Our directional microphone didn't pick up the conversation, so we waited for Parker to leave the motel, which just happened, and now we have Tyndall there checking to see if the motel security system may have captured audio or any other useful visuals because we didn't get the best view of this guy. We may hear back any minute."*

Zane felt very encouraged. He looked around. For the first time all week, he had actual agents looking out for him, not imaginary ones that Parker had lied about. He thought about finding his mom and giving her a long hug. He thought about his dad, wondering if he'd be proud of the way Zane had been handling things. He thought about Teddy, who he had called that morning with an update.

When Zane arrived, Amber was sitting on the ground with the rest of the players, all waiting to occupy the third base dugout. She didn't look at him. She had the same type of earpiece and mic as Zane. Rudy was getting ready to speak. Ches and Vic stood with solemn looks.

"Just so everybody knows," Rudy said. "Teddy's with his dad today in the hospital. His cancer took a bad turn. So, let's pray for the Rempkes."

The players looked down and waited for Rudy to speak again.

"All right," Rudy said. "Let's win this for Teddy. And for ourselves. We'll have to do it with only ten today."

"Actually, nine," Cedric said. "Sorry."

"What do you mean?" Rudy asked.

"Jamal's grounded," Cedric said. "He took our dad's Porsche and did donuts around the high school parking lot. The idiot even made a video and posted it."

The players all laughed.

"It's not funny," Rudy said. "He let us down. Okay, as long as we have nine."

"Plus, our hobbled good luck charm over here," Cedric said, flicking a seed at Braxton's medical boot.

"Hobbler here," Braxton said, raising his crutch in the air, as if Rudy was calling roll. "Even wore my jersey."

"Yes, nine players, plus a good luck charm," Rudy said. "That's all we need."

"Guys, listen up," Wilson chirped at Amber and Zane through their earpieces. *"Big breakthrough. We got Shark's face on video. I have the freeze frame, and we ran it in our database and got a hit. It's not pretty. He's a soldier that sells his services to whichever country wants to pay him to do their dirty work. He moves so much, nobody really knows his home, only that he's wanted by a dozen different governments. He's linked to some pretty horrible things, which I won't get into*

now. But for him to last this long without getting caught or killed means he's incredibly good at finishing his missions."

"Picture?" Zane asked.

"You and Amber break off someplace so you can check her phone," Wilson said. *"Discreetly."*

The other players got up and began moving their equipment into the dugout. Amber hung back until she was alone with Zane.

"Ready?" Amber asked.

"Yeah."

"Memorize this image."

She showed Zane her phone. Zane saw a large man with olive skin. It wasn't the best image because he was wearing a hat and big glasses, but it was something to go on. Shark's thin lips were smiling. His teeth in the front of his mouth were oddly pointed. After a few seconds, Amber put the phone away.

"Now I see why they call him Shark," she said.

"One more thing. Look for a prosthetic leg."

"Shark has a fake leg?" Zane said under his breath.

"Yes, and he's here somewhere," Wilson said. *"As soon as our agents find him, they'll jump him. They'll tell you as soon as it happens. Unless you see it go down of course."*

"And Parker?" Zane asked.

"We've tracked him since the motel," Wilson said. *"He's in his car in the right field parking lot, but we're hanging back so he doesn't see us. We want to wait for the right opportunity. We need to arrest him and Shark at the same time."*

"What do I do?" Zane asked.

"Help us look for Shark but without anyone noticing," Wilson said. *"Remember the codeword?"*

"Falcon."

"And don't let anyone catch you talking into that mic," Amber said. "Be cool about it. You don't have to worry about downloading anything or questioning anybody. All you need to do is play baseball and pay attention. Protect yourself and be alert when my dad and the other agents make a move."

"Or when Shark and Parker make a move," Zane said.

Wilson interrupted. *"Guys, jackpot. Tyndall got the audio from the conversation at the motel. You wouldn't think a motel like that would have video security, let alone audio recording, but we caught a break. The manager had a problem a few years back with an employee robbing her, so she had hidden devices set up outside every few rooms. Amber, keep your phone out of sight. You guys separate. You've been together too long. Tyndall is typing up the transcript of what they said last night. I will read this to you as it comes in. Here goes."*

Amber and Zane took a few steps apart and pretended to stretch as they listened to Wilson relay the previous night's conversation into their earpieces.

PB: YOU REALLY KNOW WHAT YOU'LL BE DOING BACK THERE TOMORROW?
SHARK: DID IT FOR YEARS BACK IN CHINA. THOUGHT THOSE DAYS WERE OVER.
PB: DO YOU HAVE THE REMOTE TRIGGER?
SHARK: YES
PB: HOW'S IT WORK?

Wilson paused.

"What trigger?" Zane asked. "Why did you stop?"

"Sorry," Wilson said. *"Zane. The rest is going to be hard to listen to."*

"Read it," Zane whispered so his teammates stretching nearby couldn't hear.

Wilson continued.

SHARK: ONCE I PUSH THE BUTTON, DOORS OPEN. BOMB ARMS. IT'S THE ONLY WAY I COULD CONFIGURE IT. BUT IT WILL GO OFF BEFORE SHE CAN GET OUT, ESPECIALLY IN HER STATE.

PB: WHEN?

SHARK: AS SOON AS THE RENEGADES LOSE. AGAIN, IF THE SEASON ENDS, WE CUT OUR LOSSES, GET OUT WITH WHAT WE HAVE. IF THERE ARE NO MORE GAMES FOR THE RENEGADES, THERE'S NO MORE CHANCE TO GET THE DECODER KEY OR THAT GIRL. WE'LL HAVE NO USE FOR THE HOSTAGE.

PB: SO IF THEY WIN THIS SEMIFINAL, AND WE DON'T HAVE THE DECODER KEY YET, DON'T DO ANYTHING. WE'LL COME BACK SATURDAY AND TRY ONE LAST TIME.

SHARK: YOU TAKE ALL THE FUN OUT OF THIS, YOU KNOW?

PB: WE MAY NEED HER.

SHARK: FINE. BUT IF THEY LOSE TODAY, WE'RE DONE HERE, AND SHE'S A LIABILITY. GAME OVER FOR HER. GAME OVER FOR AMBER. THE ONLY LOOSE END WILL BE ZANE.

PB: I'LL HANDLE HIM.

SHARK: FINE. PLAY BALL!

"*...That's it,*" Wilson said.

Zane opened his mouth to throw up but nothing came out.

"*Kid, don't react,*" Wilson said. "*Remember, you're being watched. Every second.*"

Zane found a spot alone behind the dugout and took a knee. He put his face in his glove so he could talk without anybody noticing. Amber stayed put and busied herself in her bag.

"We need to arrest Parker right now," Zane said. "We should've arrested him when we had the chance. We have to stop the game."

"Zane, are you even listening?" Amber mumbled into her mic. "Shark is here watching us, with his finger on the detonator. He might even have a gun pointed at me right now. You gotta play along."

"But my mom could die," Zane said. "There are killers among us. We have to get out of here and do something. Now."

"*You* are *doing something,*" Wilson said. "*You have lured them here. You have to play along until we make our move. Your only job now is to win this game. And your team is already down to nine players. Look, I know you're scared, but we've got five highly, highly-trained agents here, plus Amber and I. Two more are patrolling the streets in unmarked cars around Falcon Field. We will find Shark any minute, get the jump on him, and swarm Parker that same second. We'll get them before they act.*"

"We could tell everybody on the other team what's happening and make them go easy on us," Zane said, making one last attempt to change the situation.

"Yeah, like they'd believe you," Amber said. "And even if they did, like that wouldn't tip off Parker and Shark? We have to play this out their way."

"Wilson," Zane said. "What's the backup plan?"

"Win," Wilson said. *"I will never forgive myself for putting my daughter in this situation, and I never would have agreed to have her help in the first place if I thought anything like this might happen. But here we are, and the safest thing for everybody is to play this out and win."*

Zane stood back up to gather himself. He inhaled and tugged down on the bill of his cap. "It's settled then," he said. "We win this ballgame. Wilson, your team does your job. Amber, our team does ours."

"That's what I'm talking about!" Wilson said.

"How's the hand today?" Amber said.

Zane opened his left hand as much as he could. "Doesn't matter," he said. "We're winning this game."

POP!

Zane and Amber flinched, thinking they heard a gunshot. They looked up and exhaled, realizing it was the sound of a fastball hitting a mitt. The Bombers were warming up.

"Only one pitcher in this league can make a ball pop like that," Amber said.

CHAPTER 32

MOOSE. THE BIGGEST, meanest kid in the league.

"Why'd it have to be *him?*" Zane asked.

As warmups were winding down, the players began assembling in the dugout. As tense as Zane and Amber were, their teammates weren't exactly feeling the same kind of pressure. Sammy squirted his water bottle at Yuri, who reached up and swatted his hat off. Ricky swiped the sweat-streaked cap and put it on his own head, then took it off immediately.

"I can't breathe, I can't breathe," he said, laughing.

"Guys how about a little focus?" Rudy said.

Amber and Zane followed their teammates to the bench and tried to act relaxed.

"Hey Zane, isn't that the guy that hit you in the head?" Erik asked.

"He doesn't need a reminder," Sammy said. "Besides, it was only because Zane put Moose in his place to start that game."

"Yeah, right," Erik said.

"Actually, Erik's right," Zane said.

"Whatever," Cedric said. "If you aren't afraid of Moose, neither are we."

The players laughed.

Zane looked off in the distance. "If that makes you feel better, then go with it," he said.

"Why wouldn't they save Moose's arm for the Championship?" Sammy asked his dad. "Do they have another ace also?"

"It looks that way," Ches said. "Or they must think that we're a bigger threat than whoever they would face tomorrow. How about that?" Ches smiled.

"That's good!" Sammy said. "Except for the whole 'having to hit Moose' thing."

"We're not saving Dorian for tomorrow," Ches said. "If we don't win this, there is no tomorrow."

"That might be more true than you guys realize," Zane said.

The game was about to begin. Zane studied all the people in the stands. One guy had a hat pulled down low and was reading a magazine. Zane kept looking. The man lowered the magazine, and Zane realized it wasn't Shark.

A black man with big muscles was relaxing in a lawn chair way out in right field. That matched the description of one of the agents that Wilson had given him. Zane looked over at the parking lot on the third base side to see if anybody was waiting in their car. "Wilson, which ones are ours again?" Zane asked softly.

"We went over this already," Wilson said. *"Older guy in the concession stands with the fancy hair is Reyes. Soccer*

mom with the red Nats hat, sitting on our side is McNally. Muscle man in the lawn chair in right is Becker. Then of course there's me and the two perimeter agents. They are on the move but in rhythm. All of us are on high alert and very good at what we do. We've got your back."

"Where are you?" Zane asked.

"I'm making the rounds," Wilson said. *"I'm also looking right at you. Let's play ball."*

As the Renegades exited the dugout to take the field, Dorian paused at the opening in the fence. He put his hand up to stop Zane from passing. He looked uncomfortable.

"What?" Zane asked.

Dorian took off his cap and wiped his forehead. Zane noticed he had written something underneath the bill, presumably in Greek.

"I wanted to talk to you and Teddy, but he's not here. I know you guys are friends. Will you tell him...?"

"Guys, let's go!" Rudy ordered from the other end of the dugout.

Dorian looked at Rudy, then back at Zane.

"Later," he said, turning to the field. He put his cap back on and headed for the mound.

Zane studied Dorian for a moment, then headed out to centerfield. After the last round of warmups, the game began. The Renegades were the home team and in the field first. Dorian started the game by striking out the side. He pumped his fist as he walked off the mound to applause.

The Renegades were up. Jamal was grounded and out of the lineup, so Rudy had moved the speedy Zane to the top of the order.

"Get it started now," Rudy cheered.

Zane stepped to the plate and locked eyes with Moose, who delivered another icy stare. Zane remembered the feeling of getting hit right in the head. Moose looked ten feet tall on the mound. Zane tried to relax and gripped his bat best he could. Moose wound up and fired.

Zane instinctively backed away, and saw the pitch go right down the middle.

"*Strike!*" the umpire yelled.

"Don't be afraid of this guy!" Ricky yelled.

Zane stepped back in and dug his toes in the dirt. Even if he could barely hold the bat with his aching hand, he would try to make contact. Moose sensed what Zane was thinking and fired a fastball way outside. Zane swung and missed.

Zane was down 0-2. The next pitch was another fastball well outside. Zane knew not to swing.

"*Strike!*" the ump yelled again.

The Bombers' fans cheered. Zane was in disbelief. The umpire turned his back before Zane could say anything.

"*Mooooooooose,*" came the call from the Bombers' dugout.

Zane walked back to the Renegades bench and looked at Amber hopefully.

"Terrible call," he said.

"We'll be okay," she said.

Cedric followed with a ground out. Dorian ended the inning by striking out. "Man, that guy throws hard."

Dorian may have had no trouble pitching in the first, but he hadn't faced Moose. In the top of the second, Moose, the cleanup hitter, started the inning by demolishing the first pitch. It cleared the fence by a mile.

"Mooooose!" the Bombers screamed again. As Moose rounded the bases, he looked at Dorian and blew him a kiss. Dorian shouted something back in Greek. The game was on.

The Bombers scored again before the inning was up to lead 2-0.

Moose was even more unhittable in the second. He struck out Erik, Sammy, then Mateo. Each pitch seemed harder than the last, and the home plate ump had a huge strike zone. Out of the Renegades' first six batters, five had struck out.

"How's it going out there?" Zane whispered into his shirt.

"He's not in the stands," Wilson said back. *"Not yet at least. We've checked off almost everybody here. Our perimeter agents are checking off the surrounding areas and any place that Shark could potentially set up and have a good view of the field. Nothing to report yet. Sorry. You guys are doing good though."*

In the top of the third, Moose was up to bat with one out and nobody on. Dorian had instructions to not throw him any good pitches. He threw every ball low and off the plate. Moose stayed patient and walked.

"Chicken," he said to Dorian as he jogged to first.

The next batter grounded to Cedric at short. Cedric fielded the ball, raced to second, stepped on the bag, and made a jumping throw to Erik at first. Moose, who had been charging in hard from first, slid below the throw and raised his spikes, digging their teeth right into Cedric's exposed right leg. The collision knocked Cedric to the ground. He rolled over in pain as blood streaked down his shin.

"Whoa," Moose said, proud of himself.

Rudy sprinted out of the dugout toward Cedric. "Not the first time that kid has pulled this kind of crap on us! That's an illegal slide! He should be ejected!"

The base umpire, a skinny college kid, shook his head. "Accidental."

"C'mon!" Rudy argued. "You weren't watching then. That was the definition of illegal. And intentional."

Nick Moosen came out quickly to defend his son. "Easy there, Rudy. Don't accuse my kid of being dirty. It was a baseball play."

"Sliding spikes up?" Rudy snapped. "That's a 'baseball play' you teach a fourteen-year-old? What about when he beaned my guy in the head last week? Was that a 'baseball play'?' Ump, this kid needs to be gone."

"Nate, go back to the dugout," Nick said. Moose was already on his way, happy to get away from an irate Rudy.

The home plate umpire stood silently, 120 feet away, doing nothing to stop the escalating tension. The base umpire finally inserted himself between Rudy and Nick to smooth things out. Rudy bent down to check on Cedric.

"Is he okay?" the older Moosen asked.

"Ced, lemme see it," Rudy said.

"Did I at least get the double play?" Cedric asked.

"Just missed him," Rudy said.

"Aw, that really sucks then. Ow, ow, ow."

"Helluva play, though," Rudy said. "Can you walk?"

Cedric tried to stand up but went right back down. "I can't."

"You better leave now and get that checked out," Rudy said. "I know where you can send the bill."

While this was going on, Zane crept in from center to listen. He was also getting a better angle to survey the field. Concession stand man was still there doing his thing. Soccer mom was gone. Zane looked into the parking lot in right but did not see anybody sitting in a car. What was happening? Where were Parker and Shark?

Infielders Yuri and Mateo helped Cedric off the field. Mr. Atwater was waiting near the dugout.

"You got a sub?" the base umpire asked.

"No," Rudy said. "We only had nine to start with."

"So, the Bombers can send one of their subs over to help you on defense," the umpire said.

"No problem," Nick Moosen said. He turned to his dugout. "Tristan! Get out here. Bring your glove."

A weasely kid with a shaved head emerged from the dugout, high-fiving Moose on the way out.

"Tristan, play defense for them, then come back to our dugout when they're batting," Nick said. "Do your best out there."

Rudy eyed Nick carefully before addressing Tristan. "Thanks. You can take right."

Rudy stepped past second base and played traffic cop with his outfield. "Amber, you go to center. Zane, you go to left. Ricky, you go to short. Let's win!"

"Play ball," the home plate umpire commanded.

Dorian walked the next two batters. Suddenly, the bases were loaded with two outs. The Bombers' number eight hitter hit a soft pop up to shallow right. The baserunners took off on contact. Tristan took a half step forward, then backed off and played it off the bounce.

"C'mon!" Zane yelled from left.

Tristan fielded it cleanly, then hesitated throwing it, as if he didn't see his cutoff man. By the time he lobbed it to Ricky at second base, two runs had scored. Everyone in the field turned and gave Tristan a sideways look.

"What?" Tristan said back. "I couldn't have caught that. I played it off the bounce so it didn't get behind me."

The Renegades heard the Bombers' players crack up. Tristan smiled but then immediately looked down when he saw Dorian's stare.

"Good effort." Dorian caught the ball from Ricky.

The number nine hitter grounded out to Mateo at third, but the Bombers had built up a 4-0 lead.

In the bottom of third, the Renegades proved they could hit Moose. Ricky started the inning by poking the first pitch he saw into right for a single. Yuri grounded out to third, but Ricky advanced to second. Amber, the number nine hitter, got her first at-bat and had a runner in scoring position. "Here we go!" Sammy shouted. "Rally time."

"Yeah, but it's Amber," Erik said.

Amber stepped across the chalked line of the batter's box. She tapped the end of her bat on the plate. She looked over at Zane and winked.

Moose threw one hard down the middle. Amber turned on it and followed through perfectly with her arms. The ball sailed into the outfield, all the way to the wall. Ricky scored easily. Bombers 4, Renegades 1. Everybody cheered.

"You were saying?" Sammy said to Erik.

"Where did *that* come from?" Erik asked.

Zane came up next at the top of the order.

"Relax, Zane, you got this," Wilson said into his earpiece.

"I was wondering if you were still here," Zane mumbled.

"Still scoping the scene," Wilson said. *"You worry about this at bat."*

He knew if he hit the ball, the pain in his hand would be intense. He had no choice. The third pitch he saw was the one for him. He swung on the money and nailed it. The shock in his hand caused him to drop the bat on the follow through. Moose instinctively reached up and caught the line drive. He spun and fired to first base to double up Amber, ending the inning.

"You okay?" Rudy asked.

"Fine," Zane said.

"That didn't look fine," Rudy said. "You're shaking your hand around like it's some new dance."

"My mom said I could play if it didn't hurt too bad. Well, it doesn't hurt too bad, I just hit it kind of funny. We're good. And you guys need me."

"Okay then."

By the bottom of the fourth, the Renegades were down 5-1.

Cedric, their two hitter, was due up first. He was long gone, and they had no subs. Dorian, the three hitter, was about to go up instead. Rudy stared at Nick Moosen from across the diamond. He stopped Vic before he went out to coach third.

"You think he'll protest?" Rudy asked his assistant. The Renegades were about to bat out of order. In these instances, the umpire doesn't automatically call the improper batter out. That only happens if the opposing manager protests. Otherwise, the game goes on.

"Protest an out-of-order batter because of an injury caused by his own kid?" Vic asked. "I can't see it." He went to the third base coaching box, and the inning began.

Dorian walked timidly to the plate.

Nick Moosen stepped out of the Bombers dugout. *"Protest!"*

Rudy flew out of the dugout faster than anyone had seen him move all season. "Are you serious?" he shouted, running toward Nick, launching into Round Two.

The base umpire arrived in time to put himself between the two men.

"It's in the rules, Rudy." Nick said. "Why wouldn't I protest? It's your fault for not having enough players."

"Only because your boy on the mound there purposely took out our shortstop!"

"Stop saying that!"

"He should've been ejected!"

The crowd grew quiet.

"Fellas, please," the base umpire pleaded. "Your kids—and wives—are watching."

"Look," Nick began, "if I can get a free out against you, I'd be crazy not to take that advantage. This is for a spot in the championship. Sorry, but if you skip a spot in the order, I'll protest, and it'll be an out."

Rudy hiked up his belt and stepped closer. "How is that fair? What about teaching your kids sportsmanship and fair play?"

"And what about teaching *your* kids winning?" Nick shot back.

"You're unbelievable," Rudy said, breathing fire. "And this is unbelievable. Make an exception. Show some class!"

The umpire put his hand between them. "Calm down, please. Those are the breaks. It's just a game."

"Can I grab a kid out of the stands to bat?" Rudy asked.

"No. It has to be someone on your official roster," the ump said.

"Fine," Rudy said, defeated. He stared at Nick Moosen. "It'll make it that much sweeter when we kick your ass!"

The Renegades players erupted in cheers. Mateo and Dorian looked at each other with mouths open wide.

As Rudy walked back to the dugout, he looked over at the other umpire, who had stayed behind home plate the entire time. "And thanks for your input!"

The ump lifted his mask slightly, sipped his water, and shrugged.

"Real classy, Rudy," Nick remarked.

Braxton stood up with help from his crutches. "What a joke!"

Once the commotion calmed down, Dorian got a hit off Moose. Erik came up next but hit into an inning-ending double play. The inning was over, even though the Renegades had only sent two batters to the plate.

"Kind of a quick inning, huh fellas?" Rudy said. The Renegades still trailed 5-1.

The next inning, Amber spotted a large man in the back of the crowd. He stood and up and stretched out his leg, and sat back down. "You guys get close to the man in the back row?" she asked Wilson. "Bombers' side? Sitting with a woman? I didn't notice him earlier. He's favoring his left leg. What if it's fake?"

"Saw him," Wilson said. "Not Shark."

Amber didn't like how quickly she was dismissed.

Back in the dugout, she peeked into her bag to get another look at Shark's picture on her phone.

"Amber!" Rudy shouted. "Give it to me. It's mine."

She had been caught. "I was… texting Teddy updates. Please, let me."

"Hmm," he said. "That's actually good. Let's give her something to text about, guys."

Amber looked back at her phone. She couldn't speak since she was surrounded by her teammates. She texted Wilson. *"What is taking so long? Are we any closer to finding Shark?"*

Wilson replied by speaking to both Zane and Amber.

"Guys, I am going to be honest," he said. *"We checked every single human here and have made no progress finding Shark. Wherever he is, he's completely out of sight. Our perimeter agents are coming up empty. I don't know what's going on, but I don't like it. I don't think we'll find him in time. You have to win. And do* not *blow cover! I repeat. WIN THE GAME."*

Amber wrote another text message. *"We heard you, but are you watching the game? Not exactly a fair fight. Work faster. Shark's here somewhere! You have to find him and make both arrests. I don't think we can win this game."*

"You have to win," Wilson said aloud.

Zane and Amber looked at each other.

Amber texted again and showed Zane what she sent to Wilson. *"How are we supposed to win with just two out-fielders that care and an automatic out every time we hit the number two spot in the order?"*

"We don't have a choice," Zane said. He looked around and shifted back into normal teammate mode. He didn't care who was listening to this part. "Listen, next time up, Moose is going to throw you fastballs. Be ready."

"Okay," Amber said.

They were down 5-1 heading into the bottom of the fifth. Sammy and Mateo had been pretty hot lately. Each singled off Moose to start the inning, but then Ricky and Yuri each struck out.

Amber was up with two on and two out.

"Hey, Moose!" Zane yelled. "Isn't this the girl that hit an RBI double off of you?"

Sammy, standing on second, jumped in immediately. "I don't even know what I'd do if I let a girl get a hit off me! Oh, man."

Moose was trying his best to ignore them, but it was impossible.

Zane twisted the knife even more. "Hey Sammy, wasn't that her first hit all year?"

"First hit ever actually," Sammy shouted. "So much for a power pitcher!"

Moose wound up. He reached back to throw it as hard as he could. The pitch was fast but had no movement. Amber was waiting for a fastball the whole way. She simply timed it up, uncoiled her perfectly synchronized arms and hips, and launched another missile. The ball sailed down the left field line. Sammy and Mateo scored. The fans cheered. The Renegades had cut the lead to 5-3 after Amber's two-run double.

Zane was up next. "Amber, you did it again!" he yelled, winking at Moose.

Moose's first pitch was right at Zane's legs.

"Warning!" yelled the home plate ump.

"So, we're doing this again?" Rudy asked nobody in particular.

Zane smiled. He had gotten to Moose.

"Settle down," Nick said.

Zane guessed Moose would throw his next pitch down the middle to prove he wasn't out of control. He guessed right.

Zane accepted that he was about to feel pain in his hand, and crushed a double of his own. Zane stopped at second and tried to smile but was too worried about his throbbing hand. Watching Amber score made it bearable. It was now Bombers 5, Renegades 4 and there was still a runner on second. Just one problem—Cedric was up next.

Dorian tentatively walked to the plate, knowing full well it wasn't his turn to bat.

"Protest," Nick said.

"Out," the ump said. *"Inning over."*

"Seriously!" Erik said.

"Is that the only way you can stop a rally?" Rudy yelled across to Nick.

"You guys realize our coaches are talking more trash than we are?" Mateo said. The players all laughed, except Amber and Zane.

Coach Ches walked over to his son, Sammy. "You have Cedric's number, right?"

"Yeah," Sammy said. "What for?"

"Call him and see if you can get his dad on the line. Maybe we can get Jamal out here. He can serve his punishment by missing the championship game, not this one. We need him now."

Sammy laughed and slapped his knee. "You obviously don't know Mister Atwater."

Ches stared back patiently.

"This isn't going to work," Sammy said, fishing his phone out. He rang Cedric, who answered right away.

Sammy got right to the point. "Can I talk to your dad real quick? I know. Please. Just put him on." The team gathered around and listened. "Uh, hi sir. I know Jamal is punished today, but if we don't have a ninth player, it's an automatic out each time, and my dad was wondering—"

From there, Sammy went silent. Ten seconds later he started answering in rapid fire. "Uh-huh, no sir. Yes sir, uh-huh. I didn't mean to. I will. Yes, sir. Thank you. Sorry." He put the phone down and looked up at his hopeful teammates. "Of course he's not coming!" He looked at his dad. "And he said he's going to call you later tonight."

Neither team scored in the sixth, so they started the seventh with the Bombers still up, 5-4. The Renegades took the field.

"Zane, I am so sorry," Wilson said. *"We let you down. I promise our agents are still scanning everything and everyone, but we have nothing. Shark and Parker have had no communication since the last one we all saw. Our only hope is to win this game."*

Zane held his thumb up in the air.

"Let's get some insurance here, boys!" yelled the Bombers' skipper.

Dorian kept his hot streak going, striking out the first two batters.

Zane looked over at Amber. "We *HAVE* to keep this to a one-run game," he said.

Amber nodded.

But the top of the order came up for the Bombers. Their leadoff man got a hit. Dorian walked the next guy. Zane started pacing around.

Dorian walked the next hitter as well, loading the bases.

"Let's break this thing open!" Nick yelled from third base, clapping.

"Do you see who's up next?" Zane said. He felt panic creeping in. "If he hits this one out, we'll be down nine four. We'd be done."

Moose came up to bat with a smug look on his face. Moose knew that Dorian had to pitch him strikes, otherwise he'd end up walking in a run.

Dorian took a deep breath. He had been trying to get his curveball to curve all game with no luck. He decided to go with the fastball. He wound up and fired one to Sammy as hard as he could. Moose recognized the pitch and smiled big. He unloaded his powerful swing at the perfect time, crushing a towering shot high to right center. Right fielder Tristan didn't even fake an effort to track it. That would have been pointless, since everyone there knew it was gone. Zane felt a pit in his stomach and stared forlornly at the flight of the ball.

Amber had other ideas.

The second the ball was hit, she exploded from her spot in center, churning her legs like an Olympic sprinter, flying across the outfield.

"Amber, it's gone!" Zane shouted.

"What's she doing?" Dorian said from the mound.

Amber raced furiously, faster than any human Zane had ever seen. Her legs pumped back and forth like pistons inside a premium race car. As she approached the fence, she didn't slow down. She sped up.

And launched herself into the air.

CHAPTER 33

IN MIDAIR, AMBER rammed her right foot high into the chain link fence, pushed up, and used her momentum to hurtle another five feet into the sky. At the height of her jump, she twisted her body back to face the incoming ball. She reached as high as humanly possible and opened her glove wide. The ball zipped into the top edge of her webbing—and stuck.

She landed on both feet on the other side of the fence and held up her trophy for all to see. The crowd roared. The inning was over. Instead of it being a grand slam and a 9-4 lead for the Bombers, it was still just a 5-4 Bombers lead. The Renegades had a chance, and so did Mallory.

"That was the most incredible thing I've ever seen!" Zane shouted from left.

"Just doing my job." Amber was beaming. She hopped back over the fence and started jogging back with Zane.

"Could you have played ball like this all season?"

Amber laughed. "I didn't want to stand out too much, you know?"

As they got to the infield, Amber was greeted by her shocked teammates. Even Tristan tipped his cap.

"You're amazing!" Dorian said.

"Unbelievable," Mateo said. "How?"

"Are you human?" Sammy asked.

"Okay, okay, okay," she said, enjoying the attention. "But can we get a run? We got at least one run in us?!"

Everybody cheered again as they entered the dugout.

"I won't let us lose," she told Zane.

"Me neither."

Rudy got the team's attention. "All right, last chance. We got Yuri, Amber, then the top of the order with Zane."

"And then Cedric," Zane said.

"It's okay, it's okay," Rudy said. "We'll get it done."

Yuri walked to the plate. The players started cheering him on. He needed it. He hadn't even made contact all day.

Moose blew three straight pitches past him. One out.

Amber was up next. Zane was on deck. He looked around at the stands, desperately searching for some sign of activity. An agent moving in on somebody. Anything.

Somewhere out there was a man itching to blow up his mom.

"Wilson?" Zane asked.

"Sorry guys, we're doing everything we can. No sign of Shark. Nothing has changed. It's on you to win it."

"Come on, Amber," Zane said.

Amber looked like the calmest person in the world. Moose wound up and pitched—right at Amber's feet.

She jumped out of the way at the last moment.

Rudy laughed. "It's like a joke at this point. Of course that would happen."

Amber wasn't rattled in the slightest. She looked even calmer than before. Moose knew he wouldn't get away with two target throws in a row. He threw a fastball low but over the plate. Amber turned on it, tagging a screaming line drive to the gap in left. She was halfway to second base by the time the left fielder grabbed it. The fielder threw to second. As the ball traveled to the bag, Amber passed the base and kept going. The second baseman caught it and fired to third. Amber beat the throw standing up.

"Seriously, who *is* that girl?" Erik said.

Zane smiled as he walked to the plate. There was only one out, but with Cedric's spot in the order up next, the game would be over if Zane got out. Amber was ninety feet away from tying the score. Zane scanned the crowd. Nothing. Nobody could do this but him.

He took half a warmup swing. His hand hurt so bad he couldn't support the weight of the bat. He closed his eyes for a brief moment and pictured his mom and dad's encouraging faces.

"Ha!" Moose said from the mound. "Praying?"

Zane didn't respond. He took his dad's lucky coin out of his pocket and rubbed it. He put it back, stepped in, and put his bat on his shoulder. Then, he pointed out to centerfield, calling his shot.

"Whoa, whoa, Zane-o!" Sammy yelled.

Moose shook his head. He fired a pitch way inside. Zane twisted out of the way.

"Call *that*," Moose said.

Zane got ready once again.

Moose checked Amber at third, then delivered the pitch. Zane dropped his hands and bunted down the third base line. He took off for first as Amber dashed for home. The Bombers' third baseman was right behind her, charging for the ball. He picked it up and made a perfect toss to the catcher, who caught the ball a step before Amber arrived. Amber slid.

"Out!" the ump yelled.

The Bombers all cheered. Amber was on the ground. She looked up at Zane with grave concern.

Two outs. Cedric was up next.

"Dorian," Rudy said. "Don't go up to the plate."

Nick walked out of the Bombers' dugout. "Is that it, then?" He looked at the home plate umpire. "If they don't have a pinch hitter, then…."

Braxton got up from the dugout on one leg. "Yuri, give me your shoe." He frantically un-velcroed his walking boot and yelled aloud for all to hear. "I'm fine, I'm fine. I can hit. I have my jersey on." He tried to grab a helmet but fell down.

"Ump, that kid can't even stand," Nick said. "He's wearing jeans for crying out loud. It's not safe. They don't have a pinch hitter. I protest."

Zane stood frozen on first base, every muscle tense. He was about to start running. He didn't even know where.

"Stay cool, Zane," Wilson said. *"All agents be ready."*

"Well?" Nick demanded.

The umpire stepped forward, about to speak.

"Wait!" Dorian yelled, pointing with his bat. "Look!"

The players all turned to see.

"Amber, what did you text him?" Braxton asked.

"Text who?" Amber asked, confused. "What are you talking about? What's happening?"

"Teddy," Zane said. "Teddy. Freaking. Rempke."

CHAPTER 34

THEY ALL TURNED to face the parking lot. There he was, dressed and ready to go, walking toward them with a bat on his shoulder.

"Ted-dy! Ted-dy! Ted-dy! Ted-dy!" the players chanted.

"Agents stand down!" Wilson yelled into his microphone. *"Don't break cover yet."*

"Affirmative," came the response.

Rudy sprinted on to the field, waving his arms. "I call time, call time! Game's not over! Game's not over!"

"Calm down," Nick said as he rolled his eyes.

The umpire put both hands up. "Time."

"We have our pinch hitter right here," Rudy said.

"Whatever," Nick said.

The umpire in the field spoke up. "If you wanna use him, you better get him up there."

"Teddy!" Zane shouted from first base. "We need you now, buddy!"

"Hurry!" Yuri said. "You're up!"

Teddy had no idea what was happening but hustled to the dugout. "Good thing my dad told me to come. Somebody toss me a helmet. Wanna tell me what's going on? Braxton's stealing shoes?"

"Ced's hurt, and there's nobody to pinch hit," Rudy said. "We're down one run. Down to our final out."

"Oh, and Moose is pitching," Mateo said, tossing him a helmet.

"No problem," Teddy said.

Zane ran over from first and gave him a high-five.

"Oh, and one more thing," Zane said. "I really, really can't afford for us to lose this game. Understand?"

Teddy paused and took a long look at his friend. "You're the reason I came back. Sorry I'm late."

Zane patted Teddy's helmet and managed a smile. He ran back to first base.

As Teddy worked his way through the dugout and toward the plate, everybody patted his back and helmet.

"Ted-dy! Ted-dy! Ted-dy!"

Zane looked at Amber in the dugout. "Wilson?" he said. "Any guidance here?"

"Amber, remember what we planned," Wilson said. *"The second this game is over, I want you to run to my car and get in."*

"Dad, that's—"

"Don't you dare *argue this,"* Wilson snapped. *"I never wanted you in any kind of danger at all, and this has gotten way out of hand. No matter what happens, you run to the car. I am keeping you safe. No arguments. Zane, we'll have people on you in a flash."*

"Play ball!" yelled the umpire.

"Mom," Zane whispered to himself. "Wherever you are, just know I love you. I am sorry for all the things I said and did. I understand now. I didn't before. In case I don't see you again, you're the best. Dad would be so proud. Of both of us." Chills washed over his body.

"You'll see her again, Zane," Wilson said. *"You will."*

Zane was a bit embarrassed that Wilson heard. He got his head back in the game and looked around. The crowd was on its feet. Moose looked to his catcher and got the sign. He wound up and fired.

Teddy swung late and missed.

The next pitch hummed in at major league speed and snapped into the catcher's mitt with a pop. Teddy was even later. Strike two.

Zane could barely watch. "C'mon, Teddy!"

Another fastball. Teddy swung and barely nicked it backward to the backstop. "Still alive!" Amber yelled.

"Not for long, loser," Moose said.

Teddy was mad. Mad at Moose for being a jerk. Mad at cancer. Mad at the grownups who chose to act like kids, even more mad at the grownups screwing around with Zane's life. There was only one thing he could control—channeling his own anger into this one moment of supreme focus.

Two outs. Two strikes. Bottom of the seventh. Renegades down 5-4. Final chance. Teddy opened his eyes wide and steadied his breathing.

Moose was set. He fired. Teddy started his swing a half beat early, recognized where the pitch was headed, and adjusted his bat to low and away.

Contact.

Teddy drove the ball toward the right-field line. As Zane was running toward second base, he peeked over his shoulder. The right fielder charged at it and dove—just not far enough.

As the kid lay on the ground, the hard-hit ball skidded past him, rolling all the way to the fence, where it stopped. Zane was on his way to third. Coach Vic, over at third, was jumping up and waving Zane in to score. Zane made the turn and sprinted home easily to tie the game at 5. He looked up and saw Teddy had already passed second and was gaining speed.

"*Run!*" shouted the dugout.

Since the right fielder had fallen, the Bombers' centerfielder had to run all the way to the corner in right to get to the ball. He had just thrown to the cutoff man as Teddy rounded third.

"*GO! GO! GO!*" Coach Vic screamed.

The players in both dugouts were jumping up and down, frenetically shaking the fence in anticipation. Teddy had never flown faster in his life. The Bombers' second baseman caught the cutoff throw, and in one smooth motion turned and fired home.

Teddy's anger built into a burning hot ball. He saw the Bombers' catcher blocking the plate, waiting for the throw. Teddy half slid, half body checked the catcher at the exact moment the ball arrived.

A cloud of dust kicked up around the mess of bodies. Teddy's foot was rammed underneath, sitting on home plate. The ball was spinning harmlessly on the ground.

"*Safe!*" the umpire yelled. "*Safe!*"

Game over.

Renegades 6, Bombers 5

The team raced to home plate and piled on Teddy. Zane fell down with everybody before scooting out from underneath to protect his hand. Sammy ran around the edge of the pile, looking for a way to wedge himself in, but instead tripped over Zane, who was sitting on the ground, smiling. Sammy went sprawling into the home plate umpire, knocking him to the ground.

"Sorry, sir," Sammy said over the cheers.

The umpire didn't respond. He started to get up. He reached for his mask, which had been knocked partially off. Zane, still on the ground, noticed the man's black pant leg had ridden up. The sock underneath was covering a prosthetic leg. Zane looked up, startled to see the ump's mask had been concealing his broad forehead and olive complexion. A pair of big green eyes locked in on Zane.

"Falcon," Zane said. *"Falcon!"*

While the team continued to celebrate all around him, Shark raised his right wrist to his mouth. "Change of plans," he said. "Start the car. We've been made."

Shark reached down and grabbed the bat that Teddy had used to hit his inside-the-park homerun. He smiled, revealing a set of jagged, yellow teeth. "Hello, Zane."

CHAPTER 35

ZANE USED HIS legs to push his body back. It wasn't far enough.

Shark didn't care. He flipped the bat to his right hand, turned, and took off for the gate at the left field fence.

Zane scrambled to his feet. He could hear Wilson in his ear. *"Agents. Shark's headed for the outfield fence. Non-lethal force only."*

Zane knew Shark had the trigger to the bomb and intended to use it any second. Zane ran after him. If he could get to him first, he had to try to stop him. As Shark reached the outfield grass, he saw three agents running along the outside of the outfield fence, trying to get to the gate and block his exit to the parking lot. *"Federal Agents! Freeze!"*

Shark raised his arm to his sleeve again. "Boone, keep going around to the exit near the third base dugout."

Shark veered toward the exit on the Renegades' dugout, which had emptied out moments earlier to celebrate.

Zane saw what was happening and raced over to cut Shark off.

"*Zane don't!*" Wilson commanded in his ear.

Zane got to the spot a second before Shark. Shark was running at him full speed.

Zane said, "You'll never make it out. Just tell me where my—"

Shark swung the aluminum bat at Zane's head.

Zane jerked his neck back. The bat caught him on the tip of the helmet, knocking it off and spinning Zane sideways to the ground.

"What are you doing?" shouted one of the parents from the other side of the backstop. "Somebody stop the ump!"

The players saw the bat-wielding maniac and scattered. Amber was on the other side of the field at her dad's car.

"What the hell's going on?!" Rudy shouted. But he and Coach Vic were near home plate, ninety feet away. Coach Ches was in the stands. For the moment, Zane was on his own.

Before Shark could make a move, Zane kicked the man square in the prosthetic leg and knocked him to the ground. Zane and Shark each bounced back up immediately. Zane grabbed a ball bucket from the bench and held it up as a shield.

"*Move!*" Shark screamed.

Zane stood his ground.

"Fine." Shark raised his bat high with both hands and came down with a lethal swing—just as Zane's body was jolted backward, yanked out of harm's way by an angel.

Or by a severely pissed off Dorian Delini. Seconds

earlier, Dorian had sprung into action, racing through the other side of the dugout, reaching out for Zane's jersey and yanking him back like a rag doll, all a split second before Shark's thunderous blow came down.

Dorian was on Shark immediately, grabbing the bat, trying to wrestle it free. Shark sunk his jagged teeth into Dorian's forearm.

"Ahhhh!" Dorian yelled as blood squirted from his muscular limb.

Dorian let go of the bat and spun away. By then, Rudy was by his side. Wilson, Reyes, and McNally arrived, guns drawn.

"On the ground now!" Wilson said.

Shark reached for his pocket.

"The detonator!" Zane screamed.

Zane dove at him from behind and grabbed his left arm with all his might. Wilson tackled the mess of bodies to the ground.

"I got his right hand," Wilson said.

Zane was using two hands to hold down Shark's left forearm. Rudy jumped on Shark's back to finish the job.

"You're under arrest and surrounded," Wilson said. "It's over."

Reyes stepped over him and put on the cuffs. Shark finally stopped fighting. Wilson reached into his pocket and pulled out something that looked like a key fob for a car.

"Got it," he said.

"Where's my mom?" Zane asked.

Shark said nothing as Wilson propped him on his feet. The team gathered around.

Zane was shaking. "You tried to kill me!"

Shark gave him a blank stare.

Dorian put his hand on Zane's shoulder. Zane looked over at Dorian but never had the chance to speak.

The noise from the parking lot sounded like a firework. The bullet hit Shark square in the chest and knocked him onto his back.

Panic.

Again.

Everybody on the field started running for cover.

Wilson crouched. "Agents, who took that shot?"

"It wasn't us," the voice said back. *"But it came from the parking lot."*

Tires were peeling out from behind right field.

"Becker?" Wilson called out. "You on Parker?"

Radio silence.

"Agent Becker!"

"I'm okay. I'm okay," Becker said, talking fast. *"It's Parker, he's getting away. I took my eyes off of him for only a second to see what Shark was doing. Parker must have circled around me. Hit me with something in the back of the leg, then the neck. I blacked out for a second. Then I heard him take the shot on Shark. I messed up. I am so sorry."*

Wilson spoke fast. "Get an ambulance here, stat. Perimeter agents—Parker Boone is on the move by car. Don't lose him. Imperative you capture alive. I'm joining you in pursuit now. Put out the bulletin to all nearby officers standing by. I want help."

"I'm going, too," Becker said. *"I have to fix this."*

"Fine, if you can make it to my car in time," Wilson said, already running to the parking lot. "Reyes. McNally. You stay with Shark and keep him alive. See if you can get him to talk. When the ambulance gets here, one of you escorts him to the hospital, the other stays with Zane. Move!"

"You're leaving me here?" Zane asked.

"We'll get him!" Wilson shouted back. As he approached his car, he screamed, "Amber, get out of the car! I have to go. Get out now!"

His daughter never got out like she was told. When Wilson reached the car, he saw why. It was empty.

CHAPTER 36

THE STOCKY AGENT swiveled his head back and forth but only saw Becker limping over.

"Where's my daughter?" Wilson said into his mic.

"Don't see her," McNally said back. "She's got to be here somewhere."

Becker and Wilson looked back at the commotion on the diamond.

"Amber!" Wilson yelled at the top of his lungs.

"Do you think...?" Becker trailed off.

"Agents, find Amber now and tell me as soon as you see her. If she's not with her team, Parker might have her. Either way, Becker and I are in pursuit of Parker."

The men burst open their car doors and entered in a flash. Wilson cranked the engine and was gone.

Back on the field, Zane looked down at Shark. Reyes, from the concession stand, already had his hand over the man's bullet wound, trying to stop the bleeding. The dirt around Shark was turning a dark, reddish brown.

"Your partner turned on you," Reyes said. "He tried to kill you. Now he's getting away. You okay with that?"

Shark made a grunting, gurgling noise and closed his eyes.

Reyes tried again. "Help us get him back, and if you survive this thing I'll make sure the judge knows. Where's Parker Boone headed? Where's your hostage?"

"Please," Zane said. *"Please.* That's my mom. I can't lose her, too."

Shark smiled and coughed, spraying blood out of his mouth.

"He's turning white," McNally said.

"He's trying to say something," Reyes said.

Reyes leaned over Shark, putting his ear by the man's mouth. Shark jerked his hand up, swiped Reyes's gun from his waist, and fired into his stomach.

Zane instinctively ducked at the intense popping sound. Reyes collapsed on top of Shark. The terrorized crowd shrieked again and ran wild.

"No!" McNally yelled, reaching for her gun. Shark managed to push Reyes's body aside and fire at McNally first. The bullet slammed right into her side, forcing her to make a faint noise, like air escaping from a balloon. She grabbed her wound and dropped into a heap on the dirt.

Agent Reyes suddenly rolled back toward Shark and crashed his elbow as hard as he could right into Shark's bleeding chest. Shark dropped the gun and laid still. Reyes elbowed him again for good measure, then stopped, breathing heavily. Reyes grabbed his stomach, then looked at his blood-soaked hand. He stared up at Zane, gasping. "Is... she...?"

Zane kicked the gun away from Shark and looked at McNally. She wasn't moving.

"Somebody help!" Zane screamed. "Wilson, can you hear me?"

No response.

"They're out of...." Reyes said. "Out of range.... You need... need to...."

Reyes's eyes rolled up into his skull, his eyelids fluttered, and he was out cold.

"Reyes, don't go. Reyes!" Zane looked at the scattered crowd. "I need help! Call nine-one-one again!"

Nobody knew what was happening, or if the danger was finally over.

Dorian took off his shirt and put it over McNally's bleeding stomach.

Rudy ran over to Reyes and started to touch the wound, then backed off. "What is happening? Who are all these people? Somebody... help!"

Zane heard a buzz. It was coming from Shark's pocket. He reached for it.

"Careful," Dorian said, looking at Shark.

"He's gone," Zane said. He picked up the phone and saw a text.

Are you two using the chopper or not? Where are you? I need to take off very soon if we're going?

Zane had a bold idea—one that he had to act on immediately before he came to his senses. He texted back, pretending to be Shark. *Yes. On our way. Where are you?*

Seriously?

He thought fast. *Yes, I like to confirm things.*

Roof of Abbott's Hospital, like you ordered.

Ha! It had worked! Now all he needed to do was keep them there for a little while. *We'll be there in a few. Don't leave without both of us.*

Understood.

Zane looked around for the police. The CRU had requested every officer nearby to help them chase Parker as he fled Falcon Field. The two agents assigned to stay with Zane were both fighting for their lives, assuming they hadn't lost that fight already.

Zane slipped Shark's phone into his own pocket and grabbed the cuffs from McNally's belt.

"What are you doing?" Rudy asked.

"You know how you said we can always ask you for help? Well, I need a ride. Right now."

CHAPTER 37

RUDY TOOK LONGER than Zane had hoped to jog to his car, but once they started driving, Rudy was NASCAR material.

"Amber's still not answering," Zane said. "Did you see her anywhere?"

"No, but everything happened so fast," Rudy said.

"What if she was by Parker?"

"He's the one that shot the ump?" Rudy asked. "He's got your mom?"

"Yes, I'll explain later. Do you have Amber's dad's number? Like on our roster?"

"I never even met the guy."

"We have to tell the police that Parker's headed to the hospital," Zane said. "You call them. I'll call Teddy. Turn left here!"

Rudy slammed on the brakes and made a hard left. "Abbott's only another minute away," he said as he shifted his large butt in the seat so he could reach his phone.

Zane dialed Teddy, who answered by asking questions of his own. *"Where are you going? What's happening?"*

"Hang on, I need you to find Amber and tell her Parker is taking off from Abbott's hospital. I saw a message on Shark's phone."

"Amber left with her dad," Teddy said. *"I saw her."*

"Huh?"

"It was weird, when everything went down, I looked back in time to see her get in her dad's trunk. I thought that was their plan or something. This is all happening so fast."

"Well, thank God Parker didn't take her. Okay, as soon as the police show up, tell them the shooter is headed for the roof of Abbott's and trying to get to a chopper. He'll be taking off any minute. Got all that?"

"Got it," Teddy said. *"I hear sirens coming. Dorian and these other parents are doing everything they can, but the agents here might not last that long. Are you going after Parker yourself?"*

"I don't have a choice. Keep me posted."

Rudy's call was going through.

"Nine-one-one, what's your emergency?"

Rudy handed the phone to Zane. "You tell them."

"Hi, my name is Zane Mitchell. I'm working with a special government agency called the CRU. This guy Parker Boone has my mom hostage. He's going to take off from a helicopter on top of Abbott's Hospital. You have to stop him, now! He was the shooter at Falcon Field."

"I'm sorry, please slow down," the voice said. *"Can you state your location?"*

"Can you radio whatever officer is at Abbott's Hospital and tell them there is a shooter headed for the roof?"

"How do you know this?"

"Please just do it!"

Shark's phone beeped, signaling another text. Zane hung up on the police dispatcher and looked.

Boone's here. Says he was able to switch cars in a tunnel and lose a few cops, but that will only buy us a few minues. He says we should take off without you and circle back later. Said I'd have to check with you first. What do you want me to do?

Zane wrote back, impersonating Shark. *Do NOT leave without me. I'm almost there. Tell him you are waiting another minute.*

The reply came back a few seconds later. *Hurry.*

Rudy screeched to a halt in front of the hospital. Zane went to open the car door.

Rudy grabbed his arm. "Wait. This guy is armed. We can't just run up there."

"You can't, but I can. I really don't think Parker will shoot me."

"You don't *think?*" Rudy asked. "He just shot that other guy. And you're an unarmed kid."

Zane looked up and saw the helipad directly above.

"Sorry," Zane said. He reached across the car, grabbed Rudy's keys, twisted, and yanked them out of the ignition. "I need to take these."

"Why?"

Zane spoke as he got out. "Find an officer, hurry!"

"Come back!" Rudy called out. "It's too dangerous!"

Zane ran toward the elevator, hoping to see a security guard. There was none. He ran to the elevator and took it to the highest floor. When it got there, he got out, ran down the hallway, and found a staircase. The sign read, *ROOF ACCESS. HELIPAD. AUTHORIZED PERSON-NEL ONLY.*

Zane dashed up six more flights of stairs and came to a door. He pushed it open and ran onto the roof.

CHAPTER 38

PARKER BOONE WAS standing near the cockpit, arguing with the seated pilot.

"Parker!" Zane screamed.

The men turned, startled. The pilot began warming up the engine.

"Zane," Parker said. "I'm impressed. We do have some business to conduct, don't we?"

"Where is she?"

"I'm leaving," Parker said. "When your friends get here, tell them to call me right away. We'll figure out the transaction. If they don't give me the OIL soon, well, it's simple math. How long can a person survive on a bottle of water and a small jar of peanut butter? Or maybe the bomb will go off. And I'm the only one alive that knows where she is."

"I trusted you," Zane said. "You betrayed me. You betrayed your own *country.*"

"You want to talk about betrayal?" The blades of the

chopper were picking up speed. "My son was in the prime of his life. A life he had to live undercover in one horrible place after another. He gave up everything. For what? So he couldn't have a family? So he could help crooked politicians in D.C.? And when things got too dangerous, and he needed out, what do you think happened?"

Zane's earpiece came to life with the sound of Wilson's voice. *"Zane! We are back in range. We're pulling up now! We hear your signal. Keep him talking."*

"What?" Zane said.

"Our government never came. My son served this country, went on missions, and then was murdered, knowing that help was never coming."

"He made his own choice. Sounds like he was a hero."

"He was a fool! He was a pawn, and they left him to die!" Spit was flying from his mouth as the emotion came pouring out. "He's gone forever, and I'll never be the same. All because he was doing his best for the good ole U-S of A! Despite all of that, I was still trying to advance the cause of the CRU by making bold, visionary decisions. And I'm the one they call a traitor? If you only knew how much of a joke this country is."

Zane gave a slight nod of sympathy, encouraging Parker to go on.

"There is a new day upon us," Parker said. "Once I put that OIL out there for all to see, it will level the playing field on a global level. Information is power, and countries will have to turn to me to get it. And I'll do whatever it takes to make that happen." The pilot waved impatiently for Parker, who started to turn. The chopper blades were spinning fast.

"I know how you feel," Zane called out, giving Parker pause. "Misled. Mistreated. Heck, I just found out I've been jerked around the entire country all my life as part of one big lie. I don't need that anymore. I don't need these games. That's why I've got no problem giving you this."

Zane disconnected the plastic flash drive attached to Rudy's key chain. He pocketed the keys and held up the stick. "The decoder key. The last file you need for the OIL."

"I don't believe you."

"Before Amber figured out your plan, back when she was doing her original mission, she had hacked in and downloaded the decoder key on to the receiver. I copied it. I made the download you wanted. Before I had a chance to give it to you, she caught me, and we all figured out what you were really up to. I kept it in case I needed it. So, here we are. Tell me how to save my mom, and it's yours. Think fast. You're about out of time."

"How do I know it's really the OIL?"

"Coming up the elevator!" Wilson said into Zane's ear. *"We need one more minute!"*

"It is," Zane said. "But if you leave now, without this flash drive, you lose your only chance. Do you really think the United States is going to agree to do this trade? They would let my mom die before they gave you this list. Not me. I'll give you the list right now if you tell me where she is. Then you get on that chopper and have what you really need to make your escape."

Parker reached into the cockpit and fished around. He pulled out a pad and a pen and jotted something down. He walked up to Zane, holding out a folded-up piece of paper with his left hand.

"Hold the flash drive out in your hand!" Parker shouted. "If you try something, I'll kill you."

They met in the middle of the helipad, six feet apart, each holding out an object the other desired.

"On three, we make the switch," Parker said. "One, two, three."

They stepped toward each other. Parker used his right hand to reach for Rudy's flash drive. He was staring so hard at the flash drive, he didn't notice Zane slipping his own right hand behind his back. Instead of grabbing the note from Parker, Zane grabbed Reyes's handcuffs and slapped them hard on Parker's outstretched left wrist.

"Hey!"

Parker pulled back, but he was too late. Zane had already cuffed their wrists.

"What have you done?" Parker tried to run for the chopper, but Zane dug in his feet and pulled back hard in the other direction.

"Fine," Parker said. "You're coming with us." He tried to kick Zane's legs out, but Zane leapt back. "You little punk! I'm trying to change the world."

Zane crouched low and yanked his arm hard, snapping Parker's arm forward. He got behind Parker and wrapped his skinny arms around the older man. Zane held on, knowing his life depended on it. Parker, taller and stronger, used his back to momentarily raise Zane up off the ground. Parker shuffled around to shake Zane, moving dangerously close to the edge of the building. Zane could see down to the street, twenty stories below.

"*Freeze!*" Wilson yelled. "On the ground."

Parker looked up to see Wilson and Becker, guns

drawn. Zane let go of Parker's back and stood next to him on the rooftop edge.

The chopper took off.

Zane looked at Parker and saw his crestfallen face.

Wilson and Becker took another step closer.

"I'm not telling you again!" Wilson shouted. "On the ground now!"

Parker looked at Wilson, then back to Zane. "I'm sorry about this, Zane. You deserved better. But I need to make my own choice right now. I'm going to him."

"What?" Zane asked.

The door to the roof busted open again. Amber called out *"Dad!"*

Wilson turned.

A split second was all it took. Parker punched Zane in the stomach with his free right hand.

And jumped.

CHAPTER 39

ZANE'S BRAIN DIDN'T process what was happening fast enough. He watched as the older man jumped past him and into the sky. Parker's body weight jerked Zane's arm forward. Zane's body followed, tumbling over the edge with Parker attached. Zane flailed out with his free left hand and reached for something.

Anything.

One last desperate swipe.

A hand. Zane squeezed the wrist as hard as he could as his body slammed against the side of the building.

"I've got you," Wilson said. "Stay as still as you can."

That was impossible. Parker was dangling below, handcuffed to Zane's right wrist. He flopped his body to bring them both down. Up above, Zane could feel his left hand slipping out of Wilson's grasp. A cold wind hammered his face.

"My hand," Zane said. "It's broken, and I'm about to lose you."

Wilson was bright red. "Not gonna happen," he said through gritted teeth. A droplet of sweat trickled off his forehead and hit Zane on the cheek.

Parker was pulling down hard. Zane no longer had Wilson by the wrist. Zane squeezed Wilson's sweaty fingers as hard as he possibly could, fighting the inevitable.

Amber appeared headfirst. Someone was lowering her by the legs. Past Zane.

"I'm slipping!" Zane shouted. He felt like his body was splitting in half. "Help!"

"Time to lighten the load," she said.

Amber reached past Zane's head and torso, all the way down to his right wrist. She stretched her arm out as long as she possibly could, fumbling with something. Finally, she clicked in the handcuff key.

And opened the cuff.

Immediately, Zane's body felt light as feathers. He swung his newly freed right hand up and grabbed on to Wilson's tree-trunk arm. Then, he looked down, just in time to see Parker looking back. He hit the cement, shattering an entire square section of sidewalk and sending a cloud of dust upwards.

Wilson carefully pulled Zane up over the edge as Becker pulled Amber back to safety.

"You guys saved my life," Zane said from all fours.

Wilson bear hugged his daughter, then looked at her face. "Did Parker hurt you? Where were you?"

"When Parker shot Shark, he was pretty close to me. I freaked and got in your trunk. I figured it was safer than sitting in the backseat where he could see me. And then, listening in with my earpiece, I realized if I kept my mouth shut, I would be able to come help. I knew you would never have let me come, but I had to. I'm sorry I didn't speak up and made you worry, but not being able to help would have been ten times worse. Sorry, but not sorry. What would you have done without me?"

Wilson hugged her again. "I'm furious. And incredibly proud."

"But now what?" Zane said. "How are we going to find my mom?"

"You were hanging off a building," Amber said. "What'd you want me to do?"

"We can find his computer," Becker said. "There has to be a trail. And we should be forcing that chopper to land any minute. Maybe the pilot is in the know. What did Parker say to you?"

Zane told the others all that had happened on the roof.

"So, where's the paper?" Amber asked.

"There." Zane saw it blow across the roof and stick to a giant intake vent. He raced over and peeled it off. "It's a location!" He brought it back to everyone and held it out.

Port Dundalk Marine Terminal. F St. and 13th.
Third row. Cargo container 66.
Code 1818 will disable.

"Do you trust him?" Wilson asked.

"No, but this note is all we've got," Zane said.

Wilson grabbed his walkie talkie. "I need everybody we've got to the Port of Baltimore. Port Dundalk Marine Terminal. Get a bomb squad ready. Tell them I'm bringing the remote trigger. And get us a chopper!"

"We'll find out soon enough," Becker said. "The ride's only about twenty-five minutes."

A police chopper landed on the hospital helipad minutes later. Wilson ran on board, followed by Amber, Zane, and Becker. Wilson put on a heavy headset with a mic, while the helicopter took off. Zane looked below and could see Falcon Field, dotted by a dozen flashing lights.

As they flew, Wilson was talking the entire time.

"Don't do anything until the bomb squad gets there," he said. "Don't try that code."

As Wilson talked, Zane strained to listen.

Eventually, Wilson slid over to Zane, took off his headset, and leaned over so Zane could hear him loud and clear. "They found the cargo container."

CHAPTER 40

"THEY HAVEN'T HAD any luck getting a response from inside the container," Wilson said. "They'll be able to clip the bolt on the outside once we figure out the bomb. They aren't going to try the code. They're going to try to disarm it by disconnecting the wires."

"We'll save her," Amber said. "I know it."

Four minutes later, their chopper landed at the port. Industrial equipment and large shipping containers lay everywhere. Dozens of police officers and officials were already gathered, fifty yards away from shipping container 66. An ambulance was waiting and ready. Two bomb specialists in full gear were up close, working on the door. Zane, Wilson, and Amber ran over to join the crowd. One of the bomb squad agents left the shipping container to meet them.

"I'm Agent Finch. My partner's the big guy back there, Quinn. We can hear someone tapping from the inside. No idea how much longer she has, whether from the bomb going off or simply dying from lack of food, water, and air. On the top corner of the front door, there's a small keypad and blank screen. There are wires leading from the keypad into the container. If we push in the code, it might be a trick. If we try to disable the wires, a mistake could also set her off."

"I have the remote trigger." Wilson handed the device to Finch. "It might give you clues, I don't know."

"We'll take a look," Finch said, taking the trigger. "I'll keep you updated." She walked the device over to her fellow bomb squad agent.

"That code's a trick," Zane said. "Parker is a killer."

"Agreed," Amber said.

"And his entire mission was to get rid of spies," Wilson said. "This was his way to get rid of a few more agents. I better go tell them."

Wilson asked a nearby agent for the walkie-talkie to get to Finch. "Finch, the code is definitely not an option. Parker is a known killer. As you know, he was the one that provided that info to us. It's too dangerous."

"*Ten-four*," Finch said. "*Making progress. Hang tight.*"

The wait was excruciating. Finch's mic was routed into a speaker so everyone could hear the updates.

After some of the longest minutes of Zane's life, Finch announced she was ready. "*We've peeled enough back and identified the correct wire. Intel-wise, we're confident enough to proceed with the shutdown. As soon as we clip the wire, Quinn will use the bolt cutters on the lock, and we'll go in. Tell us when you're ready.*"

Everyone took cover in the distance behind their vehicles. "In five, four…."

Finch clipped the wire.

Nothing happened.

Zane peeked over a parked police car.

"Okay," Finch said, relieved. *"Quinn's tackling the lock now. Lock… clipped. We're taking the lock off. Lock removed. And opening the door slowly…. Oh no. The screen has activated. There's a countdown going. Thirty seconds, twenty-nine."*

"Get in there and get her out!" Zane yelled. Wilson instinctively checked his watch. Quinn opened the door to the shipping container all the way, but Zane couldn't see inside. Finch ran in. Quinn dropped the bolt cutters and turned to run but then tripped and fell on the edge of the entry.

"Twenty seconds," Wilson said into a megaphone.

Zane took off sprinting toward the container.

"Zane, no!" Amber yelled. She reached out to stop him, but he was already gone.

Zane covered the ground in seconds, arriving to see Finch struggling to drag out Mallory, who wasn't moving.

"Take cover!" Finch yelled from behind her helmet. But Zane knew Finch's partner Quinn was being too slow to get up—and every second counted.

"Eight seconds!" Wilson yelled.

Zane grabbed his mom by the legs to help Finch, who kept moving. Finch and Zane were now working together and carrying Mallory away from the container. Quinn finally joined in, grabbing Mallory by the waist to help their speed. They were shuffling their feet as fast as they could toward safety.

"Three seconds!"

They shuffled faster.

Faster.

"Dive!" yelled Amber. "Now!"

Finch dove on top of Mallory at the same time Quinn dove on top of Zane.

And then it came.

An avalanche of fire erupted past Zane as the ground came up and smacked him in the face like a heavyweight boxer. The deafening sound came a split second later, roaring in his ears. His world spun violently as the force of the explosion catapulted his body through the air. He landed in a heap at the foot of the ambulance.

Pain. Pain was good. It meant he was alive.

He suddenly felt dizzy, and things went black for a brief moment before returning. He felt around his head, neck, and chest, and didn't notice anything terribly wrong. All at once, paramedics were all over him. He felt something warm oozing down his forehead into both eyes. He wiped it away so he could see, but more came.

"I think… I'm okay," he said, slowly beginning to get up. "I don't know how, but I'm okay."

"Stay down," one of the paramedics said.

He looked through the blood and tried to take in the mad scene. Lights were flashing. People were running in every direction. He watched Finch start to remove her bomb suit.

Wilson ran up and got close. "Amber, he's alive!"

"Dad!" Amber yelled back from far away. "Get him over here. Fast!"

"You're not going anywhere, son" another paramedic told him, holding him down.

"I'm okay, really," Zane said, brushing away the guy's

hand. "Please, just gimme a second." Zane held a towel to his head to control the blood and managed to stand up.

"You can't," the paramedic said.

"I promise I'll sit in one second," Zane said.

Wilson helped him limp over to Amber.

Then, Zane saw her. His mom was lying down, already on a stretcher, getting checked over and prepped for the waiting ambulance. Her eyes were slightly open. Wilson eased Zane down by her side. He held her hand.

"Mom?"

Her eyes opened all the way. She suddenly squeezed his hand with all her might.

Relief flooded through Zane. "It's really over now. It's gonna be okay."

She tried to lift her head. Tears streamed down her dusty cheeks as she looked into her son's brown eyes. "Hey there, Zane-a-lane."

CHAPTER 41

DORIAN LEANED FORWARD on the mound, right arm dangling behind him with the ball. His fingertips rubbed the laces as he stared at Sammy's sign with laser-sharp focus. Other than a slight nod, his face revealed nothing. The Renegades were in the field, trailing the Eagles 5-4 in the top of the seventh inning of the league championship. The noise from the crowd steadily built. It was the biggest pitch of the season. His teammates around him were all ready—all except the three injured jokers on the bench.

Zane was pumping his left hand, now sporting a neon-green cast, up and down wildly. "Give him the heater!"

Braxton rolled his eyes. "You look like you could land a plane over there."

Zane laughed. "Check it out. Air Traffic Control." He started making chopping motions with his cast up and down, side to side.

Dorian rocked and fired the ball past the batter. It exploded into the mitt, ending the inning and setting off more applause. He ran back to the dugout, where Zane was waiting to greet him. Dorian bumped his fist and nodded. Braxton and Cedric each used their crutches to rise from the hot aluminum bench and pump up their incoming teammates.

"We didn't wait all week just to lose to these chumps," Cedric urged everybody. "Nobody gets out. Let's go!" The rest of the antsy Renegades echoed back by cheering and banging things in the dugout.

The league commissioner had delayed the championship by a week after the infamous shootings. Zane was grateful for the time to recover. The cast on his hand was packed tight with his teammates' autographs, and it wasn't the only thing he was sporting. Zane had aches throughout his back, a black eye, and a long gash on his forehead, surgically glued shut and covered up by a large, beige bandage. He had tried endlessly to talk his way into the lineup, but it was obvious he was sitting this one out. Rudy said Zane could coach third base, which was at least something. The attack on the field made Rudy seem a lot looser, like he appreciated the fact that it was only a game.

Zane's greatest contribution turned out to be simply being there. His presence calmed everybody down and made them realize Falcon Field was safe.

In order to protect the undercover nature of the CRU, they invented a cover story about Zane and the criminals that day at the semifinal game. Zane said he had been a witness to a robbery, and the criminals in question had attacked him to keep him silent. In the chaos that followed, Zane wound up in a car crash, causing his injuries. People believed the story and that it was an isolated incident. The main point? Parker Boone, the head criminal, was dead. Paramedics had managed to revive Shark and save his life, but he was no longer a threat. The war criminal was being held in isolation under tight security while various governments interrogated him and worked out who got to charge him with what. He was no longer Zane's problem.

Extra security was in place for the championship game as a precaution but mainly to make everyone relax. Once the first pitch was thrown, the focus was squarely on beating the Eagles. The young teenagers were once again ballplayers. And they had finally figured out how to be themselves around each other.

"Does your face hurt?" Teddy asked Zane. "Cause it's killing *me*."

"At least *my* face isn't staying this way," Zane said back.

"Point… Zane," Amber said.

Teddy laughed and went to the end of the bench to get his helmet.

"Why's your mom holding up her phone?" Zane asked Amber.

Amber perked up. "She's FaceTiming McNally and Reyes. They're moving around today. Even did some physical therapy. It really is a miracle. They've been doing amazing."

Zane's eyes sparkled with an idea. Since the umpire was giving the Eagles' new pitcher an extra minute to warm up, he figured he had time. Zane yelled for his mom to come over. Mallory gingerly got up from her uncomfortable bleacher seat, stretched her back, and walked a few steps to the far edge of the dugout. Zane looked at her, so grateful she could come to the game. She had been badly shaken by everything but was trying her best to stay strong and be there for her son. She slipped into Mom mode.

"You okay, honey?" she asked.

Jamal and Mateo looked at Zane.

Jamal couldn't resist. "Yeah honey, are you?"

Zane laughed it off. "Will you FaceTime Mister Rempke so he can watch, too? His number's in your phone from yesterday."

"Good call," Mallory said, reaching for her pocket.

"Should we tell Teddy?" Amber asked.

"Balls in!" yelled the umpire.

"What if we can't get his dad on the phone in time?" Zane asked. "Let's not stress him out."

Mallory clapped her hands together. "I'll handle it. You guys have a title to win."

Zane trotted out to the third base coaches' box.

Jamal led off the inning with a clean single. Amber was up next.

"Now would be a good time to use some of those major league skills you have," Zane said.

Amber swung for the fences but ended up just chipping the ball to third base. The third baseman figured he had plenty of time to grab the easy hop and throw to first. He was wrong. Amber dashed down the first base line with Olympic speed and beat the throw for an infield single. The Renegades had runners on first and second. The boys jumped up and down.

"Maybe today's our day," Rudy said.

Erik wasn't able to come through, working the count full before popping out to first. Then, Sammy struck out, but the Eagles' catcher dropped the ball, and the runners advanced. Teddy stepped out of the on-deck circle and toward the plate.

"It's all on you, Teddy!" Zane called from the third base coaching box.

"Me again, huh?" he said to himself.

Renegades down 5-4. Championship game. *Last. Freaking. Chance.*

Teddy puffed out his chest and took his stance. The Eagles' pitcher looked in at the sign, nodded his head, then delivered.

Teddy's swing was on point. He smoked a line drive laser beam over the second baseman's glove. The right fielder charged in and scooped it up just as Jamal scored to tie the game. Zane saw Amber running hard toward third base. He had to make a split second decision to either put up the stop sign or wave her home. Based on where the ball was in the field, his gut told him any normal kid would be out at the plate. Amber was no normal kid.

Zane waved his green-plastered hand wildly in a circle. "Go! Go! Go!" he shouted.

Amber planted her foot on third and accelerated toward home as the ball traveled through the summer sky. It was impossible to tell if she'd get there in time. The baseball bounced between the mound and the plate. The catcher stood on the dish, snagged the incoming throw, and whipped his glove down at the exact moment Amber slid. Everyone held their breath.

"*Safe!*" The umpire leaned in and yelled it again, making the motion with his arms. "*Safe!*"

Renegades 6, Eagles 5

League Champions.

The Renegades poured out of the dugout, not sure where to run. Amber jolted up and headed for Teddy near second base. The mob followed, throwing their hats in the air as they ran. One after the other, they dove onto each other in a euphoric mosh pit. Teddy Rempke and Zane Mitchell were somewhere on the bottom, shrieking in delight.

As the pile dissipated, the hyped-up players assembled near the mound. Zane looked around at Falcon Field for the final time of the season, soaking in the moment. Their families all gathered around, holding up their phones. Zane saw his mom, and a sense of pride and happiness washed over him. He imagined his dad up in the sky, watching it all happen. He looked back at his delirious teammates. His friends.

His home.

"Teddy, check it out," Zane said, pointing at his mom. Mallory was holding the phone, the screen showing the beaming face of Mr. Rempke.

Mallory shouted out over the hoots and hollers. "He saw the whole thing, Teddy. Zane's idea."

Teddy dropped to a knee right there on the infield dirt. He grabbed the front neckline of his baggy jersey with two hands and jerked it up to cover his face. His chest heaved up and down ever so slightly.

Zane gave him a moment before speaking up. "Hey, champ. You gonna be okay?"

Teddy stood up, eyes watery. "Yes," he said. He threw his arms around Zane and hugged him tight. "I am."

"I know you are." Zane hugged back. "For reals."

CHAPTER 42

ZANE DID NOT want the day to end. After all the hugs and pictures and trophies, the families eventually started walking to their cars, laughing and joking with each other. Zane, Mallory, Teddy, Wilson, and Amber were the last ones left on the field, walking as slow as can be. Teddy and Zane were talking about ninth grade football camp later in the summer that they had already signed up for. Wilson had his arm around Amber. Their father-daughter moment was interrupted when Wilson reached for his pocket to answer a phone call. Amber gave him a frown.

"Okay, okay" he said, declining the call. "It can wait."

The phone dinged.

And dinged.

"Sorry Amb, one sec," he said as he grabbed it and looked at the screen "I just need to…." Wilson froze and turned to look at Zane and Mallory.

"What?" Mallory asked.

Wilson looked down at the screen again, and then back up at Zane and Mallory. "I don't know how to tell you this, but it's Ryan."

"Well, what?" Mallory asked.

"Something about how he died?" Zane said.

Wilson shook his head in disbelief and offered Zane the phone. "No. That's the thing. Look. He's alive, Zane. Your dad is alive."

Scott Reister gets to live out his childhood dream with his job as an award-winning sportscaster, traveling the country and covering incredible stories and events. He and his wife live in Iowa with three children, any one of which may be a spy.

Printed in the USA
CPSIA information can be obtained
at www.ICGtesting.com
LVHW042302070524
779682LV00030B/267